D0805268

OVERWASH
OF
EVIL

Novels by
Joseph L.S. Terrell

OVERWASH OF EVIL

TIDE OF DARKNESS

THE OTHER SIDE OF SILENCE

A TIME OF MUSIC, A TIME OF MAGIC

A NEUROTIC'S GUIDE TO SANE LIVING

OVERWASH
OF
EVIL

A HARRISON WEAVER MYSTERY

JOSEPH L.S. TERRELL

BellaRosaBooks

BellaRosaBooks

OVERWASH OF EVIL
ISBN 978-1-933523-75-0

Copyright © 2011 by Joseph L.S. Terrell

All rights reserved, including the right to reproduce this book or portions thereof in any form whatsoever. For more information contact Bella Rosa Books, P.O. Box 4251 CRS, Rock Hill, SC 29732. Or online at www.bellarosabooks.com

This book is a work of fiction. Names, characters, places and incidents are products of the author's imagination or are used fictitiously. Any resemblance to actual events or locales or persons, living or dead, is entirely coincidental.

First Edition: April 2011

Library of Congress Control Number: 2011926573

Printed in the United States of America on acid-free paper.

Cover photograph and author photograph by Veronica Moschetti

Book design by Bella Rosa Books

BellaRosaBooks and logo are trademarks of Bella Rosa Books

10   9   8   7   6   5   4   3   2   1

This book is dedicated to Rod and Gwen, dear friends and saviors who have enriched my life.

Acknowledgments

I want to thank people who have helped me with this endeavor: Vann Rogerson, who explained intricacies of federal grants; manuscript readers who offered valuable edits and suggestions, Penelope Thomas and Veronica Moschetti. I especially want to thank Barbara St. Amand of the Dare County Arts Council for her editorial suggestions that made this yarn better, and to fellow-writer and former lawman, a real expert on police procedure, Lee Lofland who helped me with questions about firearms.

Author's Note:

Once again I have chosen to compress time and use the historic courthouse in Manteo to house the sheriff's and other offices, as it did years ago. Other than that, the place names are mostly current ones. Although the characters in this story are real to me, they are the figments of my imagination and do not in anyway portray actual persons, living or dead. I hope you enjoy the story.

–JLSTerrell

OVERWASH
OF
EVIL

Chapter One

Even from that distance, something in the tenseness of their stance, as if they radiated a smoldering violence, made me look at them again.

The larger man, the one with his back toward me, jabbed the smaller man in the chest with his finger. I couldn't possibly hear what he said from forty yards away and with the rumbling power of the ocean's surf.

Carrying my surfcasting rod and gear, I stopped and pretended to survey where I would settle to fish. I wanted to watch what was going on with the two men. We were alone on this stretch of beach south of Oregon Inlet on North Carolina's Outer Banks.

Then I saw the sudden swift movement of the big man's right hand. He sawed a quick, solid blow to the smaller man's stomach. His shoulder and twist of his body powered the blow.

The smaller man went up on his toes and then crumbled down on his knees, head in the sand at the feet of the other man, as if bowing in abject supplication.

I dropped my fishing gear and started to run toward the two men. I'm no hero type. I don't go seeking trouble. But I have a temper that's gotten me into messes in the past. I wasn't going to just stand there while this big guy beat the living daylights out of the other guy.

Before I'd taken half a dozen strides, I stopped because I thought the bigger man was helping the other one up. But what he did was grab the man's ear and twist it so he writhed in pain.

Above the dull, steady churn of the ocean, I heard the smaller man scream. His scream sounded like a sea gull.

He held his hands up as if begging. The bigger man bent over slightly at the waist and said something, and all the while twisting his ear.

I started to run toward them again.

The bigger one let go of the man's ear, but he remained kneeling on the beach at the edge of the ocean, holding the side of his head in his hands. He rocked back and forth like he might be crying.

The bigger man shrugged his shoulders, gave a casual salute with one hand, and turned to saunter toward the cut-through in the dunes—and me. When we were only about ten yards apart, I stopped, my body tensed because I didn't know what I might have to do.

He strolled across the beach. It was like he was taking a nice little Sunday walk. He knew I was watching him but he didn't seem to care. He was dressed more nattily than most people you see on the beach. He wore slacks and a golf shirt, unbuttoned at the throat, with a nice collar he had flipped up in the back.

He appeared to be in his late thirties or maybe forty and slightly over six feet tall. He moved with a smooth, loose, re- laxed walk, like an athlete. He was solid, too. Probably two hundred pounds.

I stood watching him, holding my ground.

He smiled broadly. A very friendly smile, except maybe for the eyes that were partially hidden behind small, gold-frame sunglasses. A good-looking fellow with sandy hair, only slight- ly disturbed by the breeze there at the ocean.

"Nice day," he said.

His face was smooth and not lined with any concern or care. He had a small cleft in his chin. A square chin. Sign of strength and character. Still smiling at me, he said, "Don't know whether you'll have much luck fishing today, though. Wind out of the southeast. You know what the old folks say." His smile got even wider. "Wind out of the southeast not fit for fishing."

"Your buddy down there," I said, pointing. "He all right?" A really brilliant question on my part.

Mr. Charmer lifted his shoulders slightly and turned down the corners of his wide mouth, a gesture designed to minimize any concern anyone could possibly have. "Oh, sure." He took a couple of steps closer to me. "Gets a little emotional from time to time, that's all. Overly dramatic, I guess you'd say."

The man's accent was Southern but it wasn't North Carolina. Georgia, Mississippi maybe. It was what I call the cultured accent of old school Southern Fraternity Boy accent. Only this guy was no longer some fraternity boy. He was so casual and self-assured that he reeked of danger.

He studied my face as if he had genuine concern. "Going be hot out here. You better get some good sunscreen. Especially for your nose. Person's nose sticks out so much it gets burned quicker'n just about any other part of his body."

Slowly, and so deliberately it became a challenge, he brought his index finger up and touched the tip of my nose.

Anger flashed in my gut like blue-hot Sterno. In a movement as quick and instinctive as batting an eye, my right came up and smacked his hand away, hard.

Instantly, as if altered by an electrical current, his face changed for the briefest flicker. But it was long enough for me to see the change that came over him. It was as though I was not even looking at the same person. He was someone else, changed by a force just under the skin that turned his face from the smiling good-ol'-boy Southerner to something so evil and filled with rage that it was if the bone structure in his face and the flesh that covered it suddenly shifted and remolded itself. Then his face changed back, just as quickly. He smiled, except for his eyes.

Then he said, "Remember, the sun's wicked today." The smile was now almost a smirk. "It can be murder," he said. Then he turned and sauntered away toward the cut-through in the dunes.

I watched him go several yards, then turned quickly and stared at the man near the ocean's edge. He was still on his knees but upright with one hand cradling his left ear. I hurried to him. Waves inched up toward him and his blue slacks were wet at the knees and half way up his thighs. Where the slacks were wet they turned purple.

I stood over the man as he knelt in the sand. Something familiar about him. I've lived at the Outer Banks since last year, but I've visited for years and worked here on a couple of crime magazine stories in the past, so I knew a lot of the year-round county residents. I knew I'd seen this man somewhere downtown in Manteo, the county seat.

I put my hand out to touch his shoulder, as if I would try to lift him up.

"Get away! Get the hell away!" His voice was pitched high with fury, frantic. His shoulders shook.

"Look, pal, I'm just offering . . ."

Blood came through the fingers and oozed down his neck. Blood dripped onto his cotton shirt. The shirt was light blue, Carolina blue, with gold call letters of a local radio station on the left breast pocket. In that instance I recognized him: owner and general manager of a Dare County radio station. But I couldn't remember his name. He was also on the air with a special classical music program on Sundays, a total departure from the soft rock and beach music played during the week.

He struggled to his feet. I started to help him, but he made a motion with his right hand and I gave him room. I could tell his stomach hurt from the first blow. I see movies of guys getting belted all over the place and how they get back up and keep on fighting. It's not that way in real life. A couple of smacks and you're usually done in. Those smacks hurt, too, and this guy was hurting.

I began to fume. After all, I didn't ask to get involved with this guy, or either one of them. I said, "I can give you a hand if you want it but don't go mouthing off at me. I'm not the one hit you."

For the first time he really looked up at my face. "Sorry . . . I'm sorry," he mumbled. Holding his ear, he appeared sad and terrified and almost comical, all at the same time. "I'm okay."

"You better get a doctor to tend to that ear."

He nodded, glanced around as if to see if he left anything, maybe just from force of habit because he sure didn't leave anything there on the beach except his pride and a whole lot of hurt. He nodded again, and I probably nodded, too. We must have looked like a couple of penguins standing there bobbing our heads at each other, not saying anything further.

He headed up toward the cut-through, a shuffling kind of walk there in the sand, like he didn't have much energy left. I think he said, "Thank you." But he was a few feet away, his back was to me and there was always the deep sighing sound of the surf.

Slowly, almost absently, I went to my fishing bucket and rod. He had just about reached the cut-through when I glanced back at him and noticed a woman and a little girl standing there watching the two of us. The woman wore jeans rolled at her ankles and a baggy short-sleeve sweat shirt. The little girl carried a yellow pail with a small shovel sticking out of it.

I don't know how long they had been standing there, but I know they were not there when Mr. Charmer strolled up that way. She kept her eyes on the man from the radio station as he passed her. She and the little girl stepped aside to let him go by but I saw her stare at the side of his head and draw back. Then she glared at me.

I picked up my bucket and took the rod and sand spike in one hand and walked toward the edge of the ocean, north of where the two guys had been. I looked back over my shoulder. The woman and the little girl were gone.

Chapter Two

Talk about something that takes the joy out of fishing. Encountering Mr. Charmer and his victim had certainly done that. I was totally out of the mood. But I was determined to give it a try anyway.

I stood below the line of dunes at the area known as the Boiler. It was a good place for surfcasting. The rusting hulk of a ship's boiler was the only thing left visible from a wrecked vessel, sticking up out of the ocean just off shore. The ship, *The Oriental*, a Federal transport vessel, had gone down in 1862 on the tricky shoals of the Outer Banks. They don't call this the Graveyard of the Atlantic for nothing.

As for that, though, the ocean behaved itself that day and was relatively calm for the Outer Banks. The wind was light and warm and only a few clouds smudged the mid-morning sky to the southeast. Low waves broke in an orderly fashion, lightly churning up the coarse brown sand of the beach and then smoothing it out like a giant liquid trowel as the water receded. I knew from experience the ocean could quickly turn and be petulant and churlish with hardly a moment's notice. Venturing out into it you could encounter a rip current that would carry you out to sea while you flailed your arms to exhaustion trying to reach the beach and safety.

I was using light tackle on a bottom rig, two-ounce pyramid-shaped lead weight, with two beaded No.4 hooks. In my bucket, under a layer of newspapers, I had two or three inches of ice and a plastic bag with small fresh shrimp. I pinched the head off a shrimp, peeled it and threaded it on the bottom hook. I did the same for the top hook. I slipped out of my ragged sneakers, and waded out into the surf a few feet, pausing to get used to the temperature. The water felt cold, less than sixty degrees, according to reports. It would be warmer next October than it was here at the end of April. But I don't like waders, and avoid them as much as I can. The water was clean, a jewel-like green. Waves were low as they rolled in, yet they pulled the sand from around my feet like the sand was something alive. I only went in far enough for the surf to splash a little above my knees. Using a side cast rather than overhead, I slung the rig out a good thirty yards, letting the line slip off my index finger at just the right moment. The monofilament line went singing out and the sun caught it like a spider web sailing out over the ocean. I was satisfied with where the rig plopped into the ocean with a modest splash.

But that was all I was satisfied with. Great thing about fishing is that when you're doing it, it's the only thing you think about. Not today, though. I couldn't get out of my mind the scene of those two men, and then the big one touching my nose, a violation, like a threat. And what the hell was the other one yelling at me for? I was there to help him. I didn't want to be involved with their crap anyway. Then that woman standing there with her kid staring at me like I'm some sort of danger, takes her kid away.

I gave the line a little tug, stepping back from the edge of the surf. My legs felt cold as the water evaporated, but the sun quickly warmed them. Slowly, with no real interest, I began to reel in, staring out at the ocean but thinking about those two guys and what happened, and how they had screwed up the morning for me. When I reeled it all the way in, I examined the bait, and then stepped out in the surf again and cast out, slightly to the south of the first cast. I turned the crank and set the bail, tightening up the line as I edged back out of the surf, gazing out at the ocean and trying to get back into the mood of fishing.

My name is Harrison Weaver, and I'm a magazine and book writer, true crime mostly. One of the crime books did real well, and was picked up for a made-for-TV movie. My friends call me Weav. Very few people call me Harrison. One exception is Elly. Her full name is Ellen Gray Pedersen, but most of us call her Elly. She is a native of the Outer Banks and I love to hear her talk. She has that soft "hoigh toide" accent that is fast disappearing here. Elly works at the Register of Deeds Office in Manteo. She's only thirty-three, almost eight years younger than me. She's a widow with a little boy named Martin, not quite five years old, who is just now getting so he tolerates me and speaks to me. She lives with her mother on the west side of Manteo near the airport. I'm trying not to care for her too much, but I'm not having all that much luck at it. I've just known Elly since this past August when I moved here from the Washington area, seeking peace and quiet.

Yeah, seeking peace and quiet. Fat chance. It seemed violence and even death shrouded me everywhere I went, including when I first moved here.

And another thing I didn't tell you. I lost my wife a year and a half ago. I still have a hard time saying it, but she committed suicide. Pills. It was ruled accidental, but I know it wasn't. I had seen her descending deeper and deeper into depression, a place I couldn't reach, no matter how much I tried. Still, from time to time I'm haunted with whether I tried hard enough, was understanding enough. I've had a bad time with her suicide—that she would choose death over keeping the life we had together.

There was a tug on my line, not a big one, but a tug, and I pulled the rod back to set the hook. But whatever it was, I missed. I reeled in steadily to check the bait. One of the shrimp was gone. Re-baited and cast out a bit farther this time.

Almost immediately, a sharp hit on the line. Good strike. I set the hook and had him. Reeling in, the fish felt good. He even broke the surface a bit as I got him in close. It was a nice fat croaker. But I didn't want him. Admired him a minute, heard him make his croaking sound, then carefully unhooked him, and eased him back into the surf. Rinsed my hand in the cold water.

I stood there at the ocean's edge in the coarse brown sand and studied the sky and the ocean. The Outer Banks are thin barrier islands that elbow out into the Atlantic. From a number of points along the Outer Banks you can see the ocean on one side and the waters of the sound on the other. The banks are that thin, and appear fragile on the map, but they're really not. They shift and move over the years as the ocean storms batter them, but they survive. Rugged, yes, but the banks remain pristine in many places, despite increasing development, especially along the northern reaches.

The sky had lost some of its crispness. The blue more faded, washed out now, and the line between the ocean and the southeast sky blurred as the wind came softly from that direction. Mr. Charmer was right, of course, about fishing conditions. Wind from the west, fishing's the best; wind from the east, fishing's the least.

When I came out this morning, I really wasn't that much interested in whether I caught fish or not. Always consoled myself that if I didn't catch them, I didn't have to clean them. Just wanted to get outside, fish a bit, and think about nothing else.

But even catching a fish didn't quite do it. It seems I can get myself involved in situations without really trying. I had gotten over the initial anger of the encounter with Mr. Charmer and the radio station owner. But they still didn't leave me. My natural curiosity and my years as a reporter and crime writer had kicked in even as I had tried to concentrate on fishing.

What were the two of them doing out here on this remote stretch of beach to start with?

When I parked today at the pull-off across Highway 12, two other vehicles were in the lot. One was a Jeep Cherokee that had writing on the side of it that I hardly noticed, probably identifying it as from the radio station, and the other was a rather dusty but new Cadillac. Obviously the two men had driven here separately. I couldn't believe it was a chance meeting. They came here for a purpose. What were they meeting about? Why did the meeting turn sour?

Or maybe it was sour from the beginning.

Those questions nagged at me as I packed my gear and prepared to leave the beach, head back across Oregon Inlet to Nags Head and on to Kill Devil Hills where I live.

Chapter Three

The very next day, a Friday, I saw the radio guy with the torn ear in downtown Manteo. Downtown consists mainly of Budleigh Street, going north toward the Manteo Waterfront, Sir Walter Raleigh Street coming back the other way, with the old red-brick Dare County Courthouse, built in 1904—a year after the Wright Brothers made their first flight a few miles away—squatting at the end of these two streets, facing the water. Other streets, small businesses and shops, cafes, spread out along the waterfront and dribble back toward Highway 64.

I had just come out of Manteo Booksellers and headed toward my car when I saw him come out of his radio station, walking fast with his head down. A white bandage covered his ear. He got in his Jeep Cherokee, which I noticed had small gold call letters of the station on the driver's door. He didn't see me, or at least didn't indicate that he did. He pulled away from the curb without looking, so that a car, creeping along the street behind him, had to brake.

As I started to cross the street, I noticed that a friend of mine, Deputy Sheriff Odell Wright stood on the wide, white-columned porch of the courthouse. I raised my hand in greeting, changed directions and went over to speak to Odell. I thought, too, that I might duck into the Register of Deeds Office just inside the courthouse and say hello to Elly. I didn't like to visit her at work often because it always made the other two women in the office with her twitter and tease Elly afterwards.

Odell was in his brown uniform with the silver nametag "O. Wright" over his left breast pocket. Odell is black, and his family has lived here in Dare County for generations. His relatives were with the famous all-black Life Saving Station on the banks, and his great-grandfather got a commendation from Congress for a special act of bravery in the rescue of those aboard a sailing ship foundering south of Nags Head.

Odell is about my age, or maybe a couple of years younger, but he has an older-looking face, very serious until it breaks suddenly into a grin.

He's also got a streak of mischief in him. With a deadpan expression, he will tell someone that he is one of the original Wright Brothers, and then watch their face as they try to figure out what to say next.

He smiled and held out his big hand. Powerful grip that always made me brace myself and never let my face betray that it actually hurt shaking hands with him. Years ago, in a fight I'm not real proud of, I swung with a mighty right, the guy ducked his head to one side, I missed and smashed my hand into and through a section of the cheap wall in the place. My right hand has never been quite the same. Hurts sometimes in cold weather.

"Hello, my man, the esteemed scribe."

"You're full of it, you know that, Odell?"

"Sure. But remember this," and he cast a mock conspiratorial glance over his shoulder and spoke in a hoarse whisper. "Just outlast the bastards. That's the secret. All you gotta do. Outlast the bastards." Then he laughed and clapped me on the shoulder.

I nodded my head back toward the radio station. "What's that guy's name, just left a minute ago, head of the radio station?"

"Lewiston. Carter Lewiston. Why?"

"Saw him yesterday out on the beach other side of Oregon Inlet. I was there to fish and he was there with another guy."

"At the beach? Wouldn't have thought Carter ever went near the ocean."

"He was there, and the two were arguing, or at least the other one was. Hit Carter in the stomach and ripped hell out of his ear."

Odell frowned. "Saw the bandage on his ear. Didn't hear anything about an altercation. No report filed that I know of."

"Somehow, I don't think he would have filed charges." I took a breath and puffed it out. "But the other guy, the big guy, who hit him. I've never seen him around here before but I didn't like his looks. Too smooth."

Odell studied me. "You have a run-in with this guy?"

I was about to go into more detail when the big front door of the courthouse opened quickly and Elly came striding out, her mouth firmly set in a straight line, her chin thrust forward, eyes narrowed. Her office is just inside on the left and I guess she saw us on the porch.

I started to smile and then, when I saw the expression on her face, I thought, uh-oh.

"I just hope you don't have anymore of your friends from Washington coming down here to make life miserable." She glared at me, then, with face set, stared off across the street. She's not a big woman by any means, five-two, small-boned, but standing there charged with anger she seemed as solid as brass and just as immovable. That tough Outer Banks heritage couldn't be masked by her outward appearance of daintiness.

Odell cast his eyes heavenward and shrugged slightly.

Elly turned back to me. "That was the most obnoxious, pushy broad—pushy bitch—excuse me, Odell, I've ever seen." She faced me like a challenge. "Said she was a friend of yours."

Palms upturned, I said, "Elly, I don't know what you're talking about."

"This friend of yours started off nice, then kept getting worse and worse when I told her I didn't have any financial records, just—"

"Who?"

"Said she was a private investigator. Showed me some sort of badge like you could get at a pawnshop."

"I can't think of any female PIs who'd be down here. What's her name?"

"Tracy Keller." Elly almost spit the words out.

"Tracy Keller? She's not a PI, at least wasn't last time I saw her. Heck, she's a pacifist. Works for Hand Gun Restriction, a lobby group aimed at outlawing handgun ownership. At least she works there most of the time." I thought about some of the part-time jobs Tracy had held and the PI thing didn't sound so far-fetched.

"Well, she says she's a private investigator now. You know what she said? When she came in and showed me her badge?" Elly glanced at Odell, who stood there with what I swear was a barely concealed smile. "Excuse me Odell." Elly lowered her voice, "She said her name was Tracy, just like Dick Tracy, except that she didn't have any dick, and she acted like she thought I'd think that was funny."

Odell put on a phony serious face and said, "I gotta go check with my brother about the Flying Machine we're building." He gave me a raised-eyebrow look as he left, like, "I'm letting you handle this, buddy."

Elly breathed out a puff of air. "I'm sorry." She sounded more like herself, her voice not so tight. "But that woman got to me."

I wondered how much of the irritation and anger Elly felt might have been tinged with a bit of jealousy because this was someone who said she knew me back in the Washington days. I could just hear Tracy make some off-color crack linking her name to Dick Tracy. I knew I'd smile to myself later about that, but not now for God's sake.

I touched Elly's arm. She had on one of her short-sleeve white cotton blouses, looking fresher and more neatly put together than most anyone else at the Outer Banks. Her fair skin, rarely tanned, even in the summer, was still slightly flushed, and there was a blush of red at the side of her neck that appealed to me because it reminded me of other times when I saw the color rise in the almost translucent skin along the side of her neck.

"What exactly did she do?" I tried to sound understanding and matter-of-fact, at the same time hoping my tone would have a calming effect.

Elly blew out a little puff of breath again, like letting off
steam. She cocked her head and gave her shoulders a slight
shrug. "I guess I shouldn't have let it get to me. I was the only
one in there when she came in. Bobbi and Sue were on break.
They just came back." She stopped, peered around at the street.
"She didn't leave two minutes before you walked up. Wonder
you didn't see her?"

I shook my head quickly. "I just came out of the Book-
seller."

She turned to me and managed something of a smile. "Not
like me to let someone get to me like she did."

"I know that."

"She didn't know what she was doing, obviously. Came
into the Register of Deeds and wanted to know about property
ownership. Well, sure. Here are the books, just look it up. Then
she said, 'But I want to know about financial records, too.' I
said, 'I can't help you with that. We don't have financial records.' Maybe then she thought I was trying to hold out on her
because she said, 'I'm being paid to get financial information
and I know these are public records and as an investigator and
as a private citizen I've got a right to know.' She even leaned
forward on the counter like she was trying to intimidate me."

"When did my name come up?" I wasn't really sure I
wanted to know.

"Just about then. She didn't give me time to explain that
the Register of Deeds doesn't have financial records. Then she
said, 'I'm a friend of Harrison Weaver's, The Crime Writer,'
like it was capital letters, 'and I know he gets all the help he
wants here at the courthouse. He's told me that, and I expect the
same,' or something to that effect."

"Oh, jeeze. Look, I ran into her last winter when I was
back up in Washington before Christmas. She was part of the
group of us who used to workout in the mornings and play
racquetball. She was always talking about some new scheme.
But private eye?"

"Well, she doesn't know what she's doing, but she's loud
about it. Said she'd get a Freedom of Information Act or some-

thing for the financial records. Then I just clammed up and wouldn't say anything. That made her even madder."

I could just picture that. Elly could pull the shade down over her face like you weren't anywhere around.

"Then she said she was going right back to Washington today and she would file her report. File her report! As if that was supposed to put some fear in me."

"What financial records was she looking for?"

"Not just the property records, she had that. But she said she had been hired to do a complete background investiga-tion—and she said it like in-VES-tigation—and that included financial records."

"Who'd she say she was doing this investigation on?"

Elly compressed her lips a bit, which she did when debating with herself about whether she should say something. She lowered her voice, "That's what doesn't make any sense, either. She said she was investigating—" and Elly nodded her head toward the radio station across the street, "—Carter Lewiston, of all people."

"Oh, boy," I said softly.

Chapter Four

I gave Elly a quick report on my chance encounter with Carter Lewiston and Mr. Charmer. I told Elly I had an uneasy feeling about the whole thing, that something was going on I didn't like but I didn't know what it was except that something was bubbling and boiling around Carter Lewiston.

"Be careful," I said, and knew immediately that didn't make any real sense. Be careful of what? So I said lightly, "Just don't get into anymore fist fights with people who come into the Register of Deeds office."

I saw her shoulders relax a bit. She gave me a wry smile. "Tell me, Mr. Big Shot Crime Writer, just how well do you know this—this dick-less Tracy?"

I shrugged. "Like I said, she was in the bunch that played racquetball most mornings. Group of us would go to lunch once in a while. That was it." Well, maybe that wasn't quite all of it but it was enough of it.

Elly pulled open the big door to the courthouse. "Just stay away from any racquetball courts around here."

I got my car, a five-year-old four-door Saab, and drove east out of Manteo. Lately I've been thinking that I really should get a four-wheel drive for here, especially for fishing, driving on the beach. But I like the Saab and am used to it. I can flip the passenger seat back and fit my bass fiddle into the car. That's the way I had it loaded when I moved down here last year. The bass, books, computer, a few clothes, and my female parakeet, Janey.

It's just a short distance from Manteo, across the high bridge over Roanoke Sound, to the ocean. From the top of the bridge you can see Manteo behind you and the beach area ahead, including the huge sand dune known as Jockey's Ridge. I turned north on the 158 Bypass, a four-lane road, with a fifth left-turn lane in the middle, that runs parallel to the Beach Road and the ocean. At the Outer Banks, you can drive mostly either north or south on those two roads, "up the beach and down the beach," and get directions based on Mile Posts.

I live at Mile Post 6.5 in a small two-bedroom house, up on pilings, north of the Wright Brothers Memorial at Kill Devil Hills. My house is "west of the highway," which is another directional code that means it's on the sound side of the Outer Banks.

No matter where you are on the Outer Banks, water is nearby, and the ocean's presence is always sensed and felt, even when it may be obscured temporarily from view by a row of houses, sand dunes, or darkness. It's always out there, vast and powerful and beautiful and ever-changing in mood and appearance. The nearby presence of the ocean, with its immense power, is so much built into our consciousness on the Outer Banks that I think it gives everyone who comes here a vague feeling of how puny we really are. Whether we know it or not, and regardless of whether we are willing to acknowledge it, the ocean puts us in our place.

When I got back to the house, I took a minute to speak to Janey, make sure she had water and seeds. I opened her cage door and let her nibble at my finger a bit. Then I stepped over the neck of the bass fiddle to get to the telephone's answering machine. I have a stand for the bass but usually when I get through practicing I lay it gently on its side on the carpet. I play upright bass and played in dance bands and jazz combos for years, then switched over to a community classical symphony orchestra. In the past few weeks I hadn't been practicing as diligently as I knew I should. I had worked over and over on a section of Mozart's "Requiem" last year that required constantly crossing over the strings. It was a tough exercise. And I frequently muttered an expletive as I worked on it. To my amazement, and amusement, Janey had picked up two of the words—the only two she spoke: "Shit" and "bitch." Janey was the only female parakeet I'd ever heard of who could mimic words. Naturally, she had to pick up these two words.

I glanced at the polished wood of the bass, and said to Janey, "I'll play for you later, foul-mouth." She bobbed her head at me.

I punched in the answering machine. Yep, Tracy had left a message.

"Sorry I missed you, Scoop. Breezed into town to do a little private investigative work for a client. Actually, I was a day late. Client wanted me there Thursday morning, latest. But you know me. Always running a bit behind. Think I might of stirred things up a bit at the courthouse. That's okay. That's what the client wanted me to do. On my way back to big Dee-Cee now. Catch you later. Hang in there, Ace."

So, causing something of a ruckus was part of her assignment? That bothered me. Dots floated in the air that begged to be connected. I'm not a believer in random happenings. If you look hard enough, there's almost always a connection of events. Something was up involving Carter Lewiston, but I had no idea what.

One thing I did know was that I needed to get back to work. I had been goofing off for the better part of two days, and I had a magazine piece I was writing, and I needed to finish it up this weekend. As a carryover from regular jobs, I guess, I try not to work on weekends, but I'd taken Thursday to go on that aborted fishing outing, and today I'd spent the morning running a couple of non-essential errands into Manteo. Okay, Harrison, get busy.

I sat at the computer while eating an unimaginative ham sandwich. I did get up to put a couple of pickles with it, spice it up. Got into the article faster than I thought I would. It was a rehash of three separate true-crime stories I had done earlier. Another editor wanted the three woven together showing a common thread, not only in type of killing but how they were solved. It flowed along pretty well. But every now and then, my mind wandered back to the business of Carter Lewiston and my weird friend, Tracy Keller.

Weird is probably too strong. Unconventional, and not caring who knows it. That's more like it. As far as being more than a friend, well, how do you judge that? The only incident along those lines came a month or so after my wife, Keely, killed herself. After her death I remained in Washington, trying to see how much booze I could put away. One weekend it got especially bad and I drove my car over to Tracy's house, way the hell out in Maryland somewhere. I still don't know how I found her house, or where it was, and I don't remember even driving there, but she let me stay with her that weekend. Maybe there was some drunken groping around, some maudlin, mewling attempts at sex. It's all hazy. I was pretty much of a mess. I'm not proud of it at all. I can't help but wish there weren't so many things I'm not proud of. I'm sure we've all got hauntings of one type or another. Just the same, it doesn't make it any easier that others may have them when a door opens unexpectedly and there stands one of your own personal ghosts.

Tracy had just shrugged off my showing up slobbering drunk at her house, like this is the type of thing that happened all the time. Now, she appears at the Outer Banks, claiming to be a private investigator, deliberately creates something of a flap, and immediately heads back to the Washington area.

I knew she had taken on a couple of strange part-time jobs even while working at Hand Gun Restriction: A number of weekends she ferried used cars to South Carolina for some shady character she had met; she tried to set herself up in a tele-marketing business, promising a number of small enterprises that she could sell aluminum siding or whatever it was for them; she kidded that she might go into phone sex, and who knows? She once talked an insurance broker into hiring her to investigate accident claims, but that lasted no time at all. So maybe it could be expected that she had now become, in her words at least, a private investigator.

Even with my occasional wanderings of mind, the writing went well the rest of the day and into the early evening. Despite misgivings about working on weekends, I also spent much of

Saturday on the article, and had just about wound it up late that afternoon and decided to call it quits. I showered and headed south to Sugar Creek Restaurant on the causeway at Whalebone Junction to treat myself to an early dinner, some of their delicious popcorn shrimp. A light wind had shifted around to the northwest, clearing the skies of any haze, and making it only slightly cooler, well into the sixties. I had the windows down on the Saab. The air smelled fresh and good.

I was at Whalebone Junction, just before the restaurant, when Deputy Odell Wright's cruiser sped past me, blue light flashing, heading toward Manteo. I eased my car to the edge of the road. Within seconds another Dare County deputy roared by, lights flashing.

I pulled into the parking area at Sugar Creek, sat there a moment with the motor idling, then did what I knew I would do. I started driving in the direction Deputy Wright and the other officer had gone. Part of the old reporter-true-crime-writer instinct. Wanted to see if I could find out what was going on.

Chapter Five

On a hunch, after cruising in a couple of blocks toward the courthouse and not seeing any action, I drove west on 64 toward Croatan Sound. Sure enough, no sooner had I gone a short distance beyond Fort Raleigh, where the long-running outdoor drama *The Lost Colony* is performed, than I saw blue and red lights flashing near the bridge to Mann's Harbor and the mainland.

Two Dare County sheriff's cars were there, a cruiser from the Manteo Police Department, and two medical emergency vehicles. An officer stood in the middle of the highway, slowing traffic and then waving it on. Another was stationed on the bridge. Traffic crept by. I pulled to the left and parked off the side of the road. I got out and walked toward the flashing lights.

Another Manteo cruiser came up fast, then a State Trooper arrived from across the bridge.

If it had been a vehicle wreck, I would have turned around and gone back toward Manteo. I was still curious, though, because there were no banged up cars that I could see. Before I walked the couple of hundred yards up to the end of the bridge I saw Dr. Bruce Ennis's black Ford pull up toward the bridge and get waved through to park. Dr. Ennis doubles as the county's coroner. Okay, this was getting serious. I thought we might have a jumper. Too early in the spring for swimming.

The activity centered toward the south end of the bridge in an area where drivers can pull off to fish in the shallow water.

A few yards farther south along the banks is a hump of earth that is the remains of a Confederate gun emplacement, which proved ineffectual in thwarting Union forces. I saw Deputy Wright and two others I didn't know. Then Sheriff Eugene Albright's car pulled up. This was getting busier and busier. I could hear the crackling sounds of radios in the parked cruisers and the two medical emergency vehicles.

Two medical techs brought out a gurney with fold-up rubber-wheeled legs. A neatly folded rubberized brown body bag was in the middle of the gurney. They did not hurry.

I was able to blend in with the growing crowd of officers, medics and general activity. I had gotten up fairly close when a tall, blond-headed deputy I didn't know said, "Sir, you're going to have stay back here." I smiled and nodded. He turned his back and walked forward to speak to the driver of one of the emergency vehicles. So I continued toward the end of the bridge, staying well off the side of the road. Emergency lights flashed, and I could hear garbled voices on their radios.

Dr. Ennis was already down at the pull-off area at the end of the bridge. An officer made an effort to string yellow crime scene tape around the area, but he couldn't find a place to secure it near the bridge, so he ended up putting that end of the tape on the ground, securing it with a clump of sand. The medical techs stood waiting with their gurney.

Dr. Ennis, Sheriff Albright, and the state trooper knelt at the water's edge, inspecting a form that had to be a body. The late afternoon sun cast shadows over that edge of the scene. Sheriff Albright motioned to one of his deputies, who stepped closer, camera poised. The flash went off four times from slightly different angles. Others stood close by, staring toward the water's edge and the form.

I eased forward a bit more.

Then I saw it. Parked, with yellow crime scene tape cordoning it off, was an empty Jeep Cherokee. The radio station's call letters were on the driver's side door.

Nobody had to tell me. I knew that was Carter Lewiston's body. I approached one of the local officers, a big redheaded

kid, slightly overweight, as he came puffing up the embankment.

"Suicide, I believe," he said, his pink cheeks flushed. "My
mom listens to him every Sunday. I never cared for him. That
classical stuff. Rest of the week they do okay, though."

I didn't know Deputy Odell Wright had come up behind
me until I heard his familiar voice, speaking softly. "If it's
suicide, worst case of suicide I've ever seen."

I turned to stare at him.

"Small bullet hole behind that hurt left ear and another
hole in the back of his head."

"Jeeze."

"I think maybe you better talk to the sheriff about what
you saw down there on the beach," Odell said. His face was
serious and his eyes were right on me.

"Definitely," I said. I knew this had to be connected with
what I had seen at the beach, the altercation between Lewiston
and Mr. Charmer.

Odell eased away toward the body.

The two medical techs began unfolding the body bag. But
stood there waiting for a signal from Dr. Ennis. He had pulled
latex gloves from his back pocket. He squatted near the body
and appeared to be turning the head to the side to examine the
wounds more closely. Then he motioned to the medical techs
with the body bag, and rose to his feet rather stiffly. The
medical techs released the gurney's fold-up legs so that it was
almost level with Lewiston's body, and then expertly rolled the
body into the bag, zipped it, and hefted it onto the gurney.

Suddenly a white Ford slid to a quick stop halfway in the
grass along the side of the road. The Ford was driven by Rick
Schweikert, the county's young prosecuting attorney. He acknowledged my presence with a cold stare and slight nod of his
head. No love lost on my part, either. The feelings dated to a
magazine piece I did four years earlier that depicted him in a
very unfavorable light. Well, like the neo-Nazi that he is, actually.

He swaggers with self-importance, more interested in
showing how tough he is on crime, or anyone who gets in his

way, than he is in doing a straightforward job of trying a case. As a courtroom junkie, I've seen him in action a number of times, and the way he conducts himself, especially with younger, poorly educated loser-types who are unfortunate enough to be sitting in the defendant's seat, almost makes you pull for the thugs. He strikes me as a man who is impatient with today because tomorrow he wants to be higher up the professional rung.

After that glare in my direction, Schweikert strode down the embankment to Sheriff Albright and Dr. Ennis. The state trooper had moved back. The three of them talked quietly.

A deputy had stopped traffic, assisted by the state trooper. One of the emergency vehicles backed into the road, turned and headed back to Manteo, no lights flashing. Then they waved traffic on impatiently. Two more cars pulled up, one of the drivers saying something to the deputy and showing his press card. It was a reporter from *The Virginian-Pilot* and a photographer. In the other car, right behind it, was Linda Shackleford from *The Coastland Times*. A long-time friend of Elly's, Linda started as an office assistant and part-time classified ad taker at the local paper and became a reporter this past fall.

The other emergency vehicle, with the body bag, remained in the pull-off area, its back door partly open. Schweikert and Sheriff Albright listened, with their heads bent down toward him, as stoop-shouldered Dr. Ennis talked. Dr. Ennis was in a long-sleeve white shirt and tie. He still wore the latex gloves. As he talked, he took his glasses off and used the end of his tie to wipe them. They moved toward the emergency vehicle and two of the technicians stepped back. The same deputy as before came up to me and said, "Sir, you're going to have to get back a ways."

I took a couple of steps back and stopped again. Then the deputy hurried over to try, unsuccessfully, to keep the two reporters and the photographer from getting too close. The news photographer, a tall, gangly fellow who took outstanding news and feature shots, framed a shot of the three men—Schweikert, the sheriff, and Dr. Ennis—talking, the emergency vehicle in the background.

Dr. Ennis unzipped the top portion of the body bag and the three of them peered at it while he did something. He may have turned the late Carter Lewiston's head to one side. Looking at the ear? Then I think he rolled the head back the other way. The sheriff nodded, and they stepped back from the body bag and apparently indicated to the technicians that they could take the body and leave. Schweikert said something and pointed to the area where they had found Carter Lewiston. Sheriff Albright nodded, and spoke to two deputies who began carefully inspecting the ground. A tow truck from Manteo pulled up, and I heard Sheriff Albright yell to a deputy to have him hold up. Schweikert and Albright approached Carter Lewiston's Jeep Cherokee, lifting the yellow tape that encircled it and ducking under the tape. The driver's side of the Jeep was not closed completely. They stepped carefully, keeping their gaze toward the ground.

I stood there a moment deciding whether I should try to talk to Sheriff Albright now or later. With everything going on here at the scene, I figured later. Sunday or not, I would call him in the morning and set up a meeting. I knew Lewiston's death had something to do with the scene I had witnessed on Thursday. My gut feeling, too, was that the guy on the beach, the son of a bitch who touched my nose, was the one who did this. But who was this guy?

I turned to walk back to my car, but not before I saw good ol' Rick Schweikert giving me that cold stare of his. As for getting popcorn shrimp at Sugar Creek, I'd lost my appetite.

Chapter Six

Carter Lewiston's death was a lead story in the North Carolina section of Sunday's edition of *The Virginian-Pilot*, with a teaser about it on page one. The story had also been on at least two of the televisions stations I could get with cable: one in Greenville and one up in Norfolk. The TV newscasts and *The Pilot* used a quote from prosecuting attorney Rick Schweikert: "Foul play can't be ruled out. We can't comment on the cause of death at this time. The investigation is continuing. The body is being sent to Chapel Hill for an autopsy." And he left it at that.

Hell, two bullet holes in his head and foul play can't be ruled out?

The Pilot's account went on to give background about Carter Lewiston. He was a native of West Virginia but had lived on the Outer Banks for almost thirty years, and had been affiliated with the radio station most of that time, purchasing controlling interest in it almost ten years earlier. The paper noted, too, that he headed one of the three groups competing to bring a television station to the Outer Banks, as well as other business ventures. "He leaves two grown children . . . a former wife. He was active in civic affairs. Although not a musician, he was a great fan of classical music and worked to bring classical performances to the Outer Banks. . . ."

It was a warm enough morning that I went out on the porch that runs across the front of my little house to sit and drink another cup of coffee. I browsed through the rest of the paper, but put it down. I couldn't get Carter Lewiston off my mind.

Naturally I thought of Mr. Charmer, there on the beach. From what little I knew about Carter Lewiston, he seemed to be the last person you'd think would be mixed up in something potentially deadly. Then there was the matter of young Dickless Tracy, our so-called private investigator, doing a clumsy, heavy-handed background on Carter Lewiston. And who hired her?

I thought about trying to get in touch with my friend, T. (for Thomas) Ballsford Twiddy, an agent with the State Bureau of Investigation, to mull over with him what little I knew. Although frequently working this area, he lived inland on the other side of Elizabeth City. I talked with him briefly a couple of weeks ago, and although he wouldn't give any details about it, I knew he was working on something with federal guys in Norfolk, not far across the state line. His nickname is "Balls," which he picked up for a single-handed arrest he made a few years ago inside one of the roughest juke joints in Eastern North Carolina. I heard about it and commented, "Anybody'd make an arrest like that would have to have two sets of balls." Ballsford said, "That's me. Ol' Four-Balls Twiddy." The nickname stuck.

But Balls is not involved in this, at least not yet.

I checked the time. Just before nine o'clock. Time to call Sheriff Albright. As I got up to go back inside, the phone rang.

"Uh, Mr. Weaver? Harrison? This is . . . uh . . . Eugene Albright. Sheriff Alright."

I'd recognized his voice immediately. "I was just getting ready to call you."

"Uh, good. It's not too early then. I wonder if you'd mind coming down to the courthouse this morning. Something we'd like to discuss with you."

I agreed, of course. But it did give me a bit of a pause.

Then I figured that Deputy Wright had mentioned the event on the beach I'd witnessed. But I wasn't totally sure. And the "we" the sheriff mentioned threw me off a bit.

Less than forty minutes later I parked beside the old courthouse in downtown Manteo and tapped on the locked side door just as a deputy was coming out.

"Sheriff wants to see me."

He nodded and I went up the back stairs to the sheriff's office on the second floor.

Sheriff Albright is a big man, edging toward portly, with a large, expressive face that frequently appears to register all of the hurts of mankind he sees. He is one of the kindest men I know, and spends more time trying to guide and counsel residents of the county than he does in arresting them. Some have criticized him for this, but I'd throw my lot in with him.

Sheriff Albright sat hunched like a big bear behind his desk, a pained, uncomfortable caste to his face.

But what brought me up short was Rick Schweikert.

The prosecuting attorney sat in a chair to the left of the sheriff's desk, tilting the chair back slightly on its rear legs. No smile, just his lips expressing something he considered unpleasant—me.

This was not a good way to start a Sunday morning.

Schweikert wore one of his stiffly starched white dress shirts that everyone knew he pressed himself because he didn't trust the laundry or his wife to do them to suit him. The shirt fit tightly across his shoulders and chest.

The sheriff bobbed his head, and indicated the chair in front of his desk.

"Sure 'preciate you coming in this morning," Albright said.

Schweikert let his chair continue to balance on its back legs, one arm on Albright's desk. "Let's get right to it, if you don't mind, Sheriff." He let the chair bump to all four legs. "Tell us what you know about Carter Lewiston's death."

I stared at him a moment, eye-to-eye, without saying a word. Then I turned to Albright, who glanced at me and then down at his desk. "Sheriff, mind telling me what this is all about?"

Before Albright could speak, Schweikert shot back, "You were right there when we fished his body out. Tell us how you think he died."

Levelly, I said, "I heard rumors while I was there. Two bullets to the head. But other than that, I haven't got the slightest idea." I turned back to Albright, "Sheriff, I was just about to call you this morning—"

Schweikert broke in again, "What was it you had against the man?"

"I don't—didn't—even know him."

"Really?" Schweikert said, that smirk on his face. "Then what were you doing fighting with him? On the beach south of Oregon Inlet Thursday?"

"Fighting with him?" I said, my voice rising slightly in disbelief. "I was down there to go fishing and he—"

"I got to tell you, Weaver, a witness came forward. Soon as she read about it in the papers. Called me early this morning. She knows you, or at least knows who you are. From all of that publicity last summer when you got yourself involved in our investigation, the slaying of that unfortunate young woman from *The Lost Colony*."

I looked right at Schweikert as he talked. Publicity. That's part of the reason for a burr under his saddle. Someone else in the limelight.

He said, "She saw you fighting with Lewiston. Said he was down on the beach on his knees, practically right in the surf, like he was begging you not to hurt him anymore."

"Oh, Jesus." I turned to Albright. "That's what I was going to call you about, Sheriff. I told Deputy Wright yesterday that I needed to talk to you."

"You haven't answered my question, Weaver."

I twisted in my chair to face Schweikert. "Shut up. Just shut up."

That stunned him momentarily.

"Now, gentlemen," Albright said.

"Sheriff, after I saw that Carter Lewiston was dead, I wanted to call you to tell you what I saw down at the Boiler on Thursday."

"Yeah, I'd like to hear this, too," Schweikert said.

The sheriff sighed and turned to Schweikert. "If you'll just be quiet and let him talk, I think we'll hear what he has to say."

Schweikert's neck colored. He clinched his mouth so that I could see the cords in his jaw working. But he kept quiet. There was anger in that man that I didn't like.

"I drove down to the Boiler Thursday to surfcast. There were two cars there at the parking area when I got there. One was a Cadillac, fairly new. The other a Jeep Cherokee. And when I crossed over the dunes I saw two guys right at the edge of the water, talking. Or arguing really."

Schweikert, with his upper lip twisted sardonically, said, "How'd you know they were arguing if you just came over the dunes and probably seventy-five yards away?"

The sheriff held a palm up toward Schweikert.

"Because the big guy hit Carter Lewiston in the stomach. That was a pretty good indication that something was going on, wouldn't you say?"

"Thought you didn't know Carter."

"I didn't. Found out who he was later. But then the big guy is standing over him while Carter Lewiston is down on his knees in the sand, right at the edge of the water, and this guy grabs Lewiston's ear and twists it. Really hard."

"If you're standing away from them, how'd you know how hard?

I took a breath and held it a moment to keep from saying something else to Schweikert. "I started to run down there but the big guy let him go and walked toward me, like he was leaving. I asked him what was going on and he just tried to fluff it off."

The sheriff watched me as I talked. Schweikert squirmed, ready to say something, but the sheriff cocked his head toward him and Schweikert settled back.

Then I told about going to Lewiston to offer help. I turned toward Schweikert, "And I saw his goddamn ear was bleeding. That's how I knew how hard." I turned back to the sheriff. "He got almost belligerent about not wanting any help, and for me to get away. Whether he didn't want anybody to see him like that, or wasn't sure about me, or what, I don't know. So I backed off. He got up and I turned and saw a woman and a kid watching from the cut-through at the sand dunes." I turned to

Schweikert. "Maybe that's your witness. Came on the scene after everything was over."

Schweikert puffed out an air of disbelief. "You tell it real good, Harrison."

Sheriff Albright said, "You have any idea who the other man was?"

"I've never seen him before, Sheriff. I can describe him, though. He got right up in my face." I didn't tell them about his putting his finger on my nose. "Almost threatening."

"The mystery man," Schweikert sneered. "You know that's real strange. A mystery man comes out on the beach and beats up Carter Lewiston, and Carter Lewiston's never had anybody fuss with him I know of."

"Then why would I be after him? I went down to the beach by myself with my fishing gear, and the two of them were already there when I get there, and not dressed at all for the beach."

Schweikert leaned forward again, his left arm extended on Sheriff Albright's desk. "What I find really interesting about you, Harrison, is that you keep showing up when somebody gets killed. You come here to write about that first girl in *The Lost Colony* who gets murdered. Then you are here this past summer when that other girl from the show was killed. Just happen to show up the very day her body is found. Then, lo and behold, you kill the local man who is supposed to be the girl's killer."

"*Was* the killer, Rick," Albright corrected. "No question about that."

Schweikert referred to the first magazine piece I did four—now almost five—years earlier about a cast member of the long-running *Lost Colony* outdoor drama who was strangled and dumped in the sound. This was when I was first introduced to the Outer Banks. I came back several times after that, and then four years later, really seeking peace and quiet, I arrived to make my home here just when the body of a second young woman was found murdered in much the same way. I got involved in the investigation and almost got myself—and Elly—killed as I confronted the killer.

"Okay," Schweikert conceded, "but Harrison here always manages to be around where there's some violence and killing."

"My last name is Weaver. It's Harrison Weaver."

"Oh, sorry, *Mister* Weaver." He leaned back. He had a way of rolling his shoulders, as if loosening the knot of muscles. "Tell me, where were you Friday night? Just curious, you know."

"I was home, working."

"Really? Spending Friday night at home alone working? Thought you might be over at the Pedersen girl's."

Nothing in a small town goes unnoticed by the locals. I clenched my teeth and now I felt *my* jaw muscles working. I didn't tell him that Elly, her son, and mother had gone to Wilson for the weekend to see Elly's grandmother. None of his damn business. "I said I was home working, alone."

Our eyes locked, unblinking.

He said, "Another thing. You got a handgun?"

"Why? You in the market?"

"Don't get smart with me. That's not smart."

"Okay, now," the sheriff said.

"Matter of fact I do. Registered and all." Actually I wasn't sure it was properly registered since I was now living in North Carolina. I had bought it in Virginia shortly after that last incident at *The Lost Colony* Schweikert referred to, and had filled out the papers at that time.

"What kind of handgun?"

"An old one."

"What caliber, Mister Weaver?"

"Thirty-two, short-barrel revolver."

"You don't own—or have access to—a neat little .22 caliber popper?"

"Where are you trying to go with this?"

"Our very peaceful Mr. Carter Lewiston, respected citizen, was shot with a .22 caliber handgun, up close, our preliminary autopsy shows. Then he was dumped in Croatan Sound, after he was good and dead, Dr. Ennis surmises. You know where he was shot, Mister Weaver?"

"Told you, I have no idea how he died." But Deputy Wright had told me, and I remembered Schweikert, the sheriff and Dr. Ennis standing there at the ambulance with the body, turning the head to one side to inspect what I figured was a wound. So I did have more than an idea, actually.

"He was shot right behind that ear that was all bandaged up. That ear you said you saw this mystery man twisting." He shook his head, jaw working. "And he was also shot in the back of the head." He shook his head again. "I don't know how you do it, Mister Weaver. Not enough that you write about violence. You always seem to show up around violence. Really strange."

I stood up. "Sheriff, if there's anything you need to talk with me about I'll be happy to—"

Schweikert broke in, "You're not planning on leaving the county, are you?"

I wheeled toward Schweikert, glaring at that insolent curled mouth. "Screw you, Schweikert," I said.

Sheriff Albright shook his head sadly, holding up both hands, palms forward, as a signal for us to cool it.

Chapter Seven

I waited outside the courthouse by the side entrance on Budleigh Street. I figured Sheriff Albright would come out to go next door to Angie's for his morning coffee, a ritual for the courthouse and town crowd for years, even though the restaurant had changed hands at least three times. He came ambling out the side door with one of his deputies. When he saw me standing near the curb he nodded to his deputy to go on into the restaurant.

He came up to me, raised his eyebrows, waiting for me to speak.

"Sheriff, you know I'm not trying to tell you how to conduct an investigation, and I don't have the slightest idea who that guy was who was out on the beach with Carter Lewiston, but they had some business together, and they'd gone to a lot of trouble to be a long way out of downtown to do it."

The sheriff just nodded and kept his eyes on me. Not being unpleasant. Just looking and listening.

"Somebody at the radio station, his secretary or somebody, should know where he was going on Thursday when he went to the beach, and who he was with or meeting." I didn't tell the sheriff that I saw Carter Lewiston on Friday leaving the station. Even in my own mind, it sounded like I was running into him a lot. Besides, the staff at the station had probably already filled him in on his whereabouts on Thursday and Friday, the last days of his life.

"Son, we're checking that, and a whole lot of other things, too." Then, as if to show me that we were still on something of a personal, if not really close, man-to-man relationship that went back a few years, he said, "Your SBI friend, Agent Twiddy, is coming down late on Monday, give us a hand, too."

I was surely glad to hear that.

Albright said, "Talked to him Saturday night. He's working something else, but be here a while anyway." He turned to go into Angie's, stopped, and came back to me. "Appreciate it if you don't say anything about what Mr. Lewiston was shot with. That's not in the papers yet." He allowed himself something of a chuckle that made his stomach bounce a bit. "Way Rick Schweikert is carrying on, though, I suspect everybody in the county knows by now." His big face got serious again. "I'm not speaking out of turn by telling you this. You know it anyway, but our Mr. Schweikert is out to get you. I know it started with that article you wrote that wasn't too complimentary about him. And maybe it's partly just politics and ambition, but he's got you in his sights." Albright took a deep breath, exhaled as he turned to go, "And he'd love to pull the trigger."

I wanted to speak to Elly, tell her about the morning's encounter with Schweikert. But I knew she wouldn't be back until that night. I wanted to get with her before she said anything about Tracy Keller's "investigating" Carter Lewiston. Tracy might very well be the link that would get me out from under Schweikert' suspicion. I knew he'd love to pin something on me, or at least to cause me grief.

On the way back to my house, I noticed again what a bright, clear day it had turned out to be. Sky was washed and bluer as it got closer to noon. Maybe sort of a ritual, but after I crossed the bridge and the causeway, I cut over from the Bypass to the Beach Road and drove up to the Kill Devil Hills beach house to check out the ocean. A wooden walkway stretches almost fifty yards from the wooden bathhouse to a gazebo overlooking the beach and the ocean. I stood there, checking on the mood of the ocean. I had the place to myself.

Tide was coming in, but peacefully. The westerly wind helped flatten the ocean. Still, the roar was there, and low ridges of foamy white surf broke on the brown sand, and raced back. Stiff-legged little sandpipers chased the receding surf, pecking as they went.

I watched the ocean for a while. What was it for me, a sort of homage? Maybe it was what I had instead of a church pew.

I took one more look at the ocean, where it formed a clear line against the sky at the horizon. As I walked back to the car, a steady wind felt fresh on my face. Too early in the season to bring mosquitoes or even those biting May flies in from the marshes.

My little house, up on stilts, at the end of the cul-de-sac, has wood siding, painted light bluish-gray. Three pine trees and an empty lot on one side give the house a degree of privacy. I had some darker blue shutters put up, and that dresses the house up quite a bit. I have a flag and a windsock on the porch. The flag depicts a blue and yellow duck in flight on a now-faded light blue field. I thought it was pretty at the time, so now I stubbornly keep it flying. Living room and kitchen open as one large area, two bedrooms, one bath. I tried to use one of the bedrooms as an office, with a desk, file cabinet and all. But I ended up doing most of my writing on a laptop on the dinette table in the front so I can look out the window and watch the sun as it moves from east to west across the southern sky, and watch the birds at a feeder I've got suspended from the porch railing.

As for the article I was finishing up, I read through it on hard copy one last time. This editor wanted hard copy mailed, along with a disk with an electronic backup. I would get the package off in the morning.

At precisely 8:30 that night I called Elly. She answered on the second ring.

Her voice sounded troubled. "I saw *The Virginian-Pilot* . . . about Carter Lewiston." she said. "When we walked in the house tonight Ethel was calling to tell me the news."

I said I wanted to talk to her privately about what happened at the courthouse with Tracy Keller doing that crazy investigation on Carter Lewiston.

She said she'd met me at Ralph's for coffee in the morning at 9:30.

Ralph's was more of a hotdog luncheon place, and not part of the mid-morning coffee break scene. Ralph's is across the street from the front of the courthouse, only three doors down from Lewiston's radio station. As I walked across the street that morning I saw the big white wreath affixed to the front door of the radio station. There was a typed note underneath the wreath.

I was inside Ralph's when Elly left the courthouse and crossed the street. I saw her glance at the wreath.

This morning she wore tailored light gray slacks, a white cotton polo shirt and her dark blue jacket. With her trim waist and long thighs she could wear slacks very well. As always, she looked scrubbed and neat and well put-together.

We sat with our coffee in the last booth. I started to tell her about being asked to come talk to Sheriff Albright.

She reached her right hand across the table. "I know. Ethel called me again first thing this morning." Ethel, who has been in the courthouse with the Sheriff's Office for probably thirty years, and served under the "old" sheriff, the one before Albright, could alternate between being crusty or motherly. I kidded with her and spent time talking to her. She confided to me that she was never, ever, going to try to go on another diet as long as she lived, and she shuffled around the courthouse on bad ankles and knees.

Ralph brought two cups of coffee.

"Want to split a doughnut?" Elly asked. To be no bigger than she was, she had the appetite of a growing teenage boy.

"Sure." Ralph was close enough to hear us and I held up two fingers. He brought the doughnuts and then went back up front toward the cash register.

Elly made a little face, sticking her tongue out. "These aren't real fresh." But she kept eating it, using her coffee spoon to cut the doughnut into small sections.

"Our dedicated county prosecutor thinks I may be involved in some way with Lewiston's death."

Elly nodded, "I know," she mouthed past a bite of doughnut. "He's an arrogant ass."

"Elly, how many people know about that incident Friday? The Keller woman coming in, doing an investigation on Carter Lewiston?"

Elly carefully wiped her fingers with the paper napkin, tested the stickiness on one finger, gave it a quick touch with the tip of her tongue, wiped again, and looked up at me. "No one."

"Good."

"I went off about your friend and that I thought she was a phony, but I didn't say who she was investigating. Glad I didn't. Soon as I heard about Carter Lewiston, I wanted to talk to you before I talked to anyone else."

"She's a key. Don't think she had anything to do with Lewiston's death, not directly, anyway. But whoever hired her might have."

Elly nodded. I could see her mind working as she studied her doughnut, a hint of a line between her eyebrows. I knew she struggled a bit with her memory of the clash with Tracy, and any possible relationship I might have with this woman. I knew she was confident in her own ability to rise above nagging feelings of jealousy concerning my previous life. Elly guarded her emotions well, too well at times. Her outbreak at the courthouse over Tracy was uncharacteristic of her. Sometimes I wished she didn't guard her feelings so well. I wanted her to—I don't know—be more willing to not hold back so much from me. There was still that veiled barrier to keep from being hurt.

I sat there thinking a moment, mulling over my emotions. In my gut I knew I should get in touch with Sheriff Albright. But I hesitated. Maybe I rationalized when I told myself it wasn't ego, that in fact it made sense for me to try to find Tracy Keller and question her, then give that information to him. If I went to Sheriff Albright now, and Schweikert got hold of the information, as he would, there'd be a big flurry as they searched for Tracy. Get her all involved when all I needed was the name of who hired her and why.

Elly turned her face up toward me, studied my eyes. There was still that hint of a crease between her eyebrows. "You're going looking for her, aren't you?"

Now it was my turn to nod.

Chapter Eight

By close to eleven that morning, even after swinging by the post office at Nags Head to mail my article, I was back at my house. I found Tracy Keller's work number and home number in one of the pocket appointment books in the bottom of my desk. I dialed her work number at Hand Gun Restriction.

"I'm sorry but Tracy's not in today."

"This is a friend of hers. Long distance. She does still work there?"

"Oh, yes. But she's out sick today."

I dialed the home number in Maryland. It rang four times and I thought maybe an answering machine would kick in. Another ring. The receiver was picked up with a slight fumble, almost dropped. Then a voice, a weak, "Hello?"

"Tracy, that you? This is Harrison Weaver."

There was a slight intake of breath, and I think she said, "Oh," sadly, like she was on the verge of tears.

This was not the Tracy Keller, full of piss and vinegar, I knew. "You okay? They tell me at work you're sick. Don't sound good."

A pause, a long one. I was about to speak again, when she said, "Not the greatest, Weav. Where are you?"

"I'm still down at the Outer Banks. I thought I might see you when . . ."

"Oh," she said again. It was sad sound, more like a sob than a word.

"I need to talk to you. About the—" I wasn't sure what to call it. "—the work you were doing down here."

"No. I can't talk about that."

Was I mistaken, was that fear in her voice? "I just wanted to know . . ."

"Not over the phone." She almost whispered. If she worried about a phone tap, whispering wouldn't do any good.

I decided to flush her out a bit: "That man, Carter Lewiston, was killed."

A pause, then she said, "Please, Weav, I can't talk about this. I don't know anything about it." There was no surprise in her voice at all, just weakness, and a tinge of fear I'd never heard in her voice.

If she wouldn't talk on the phone, I knew I had to get up there. "Tracy, let me come see you."

"A number. Give me a number. I'll call."

I gave her my home and cell phone numbers. "When?"

"Later. Not too long."

She hung up. I sat there several minutes. The call worried me, of course, but it also depressed me. She sounded so shattered. I made myself go back to the dinette table and answer a couple of letters. I wrote a check well ahead of the due date for the Kill Devil Hills quarterly water bill. I kept looking at my watch. It was almost two o'clock in the afternoon when the phone rang. I jumped up and answered as the first ring ended.

I heard the computer pause before a cheery female human voice came on, getting my name backwards, "Mr. Harrison, how are you today?"

"The name's Weaver and I'm not interested." Sad state of affairs, I thought, when telemarketing has reached the Outer Banks.

I thought about calling Elly to tell her about the conversation with Tracy, but didn't want to tie up my phone, and besides, I figured it would take more than just a minute to do a proper job of telling. It might not be that easy a sell.

At two minutes after three—CNN Headline News had just started a cycle—the phone rang. I hit the mute button on the TV remote.

"Weav?" I could hear road traffic in the background. She was calling from a pay phone.

"Yeah? Where are you? Can you talk now?"

"I don't want to stay here."

I wasn't sure whether she meant the actual place from which she was calling, or the entire area. "What's wrong, Tracy?"

"I may have gotten myself in trouble, finally." There was a little laugh, a hint of the Tracy I knew.

I gave her a moment to see if she would say anything else. I heard more vehicle traffic. I said, "I need to know who hired you for down here."

Fear was back in her voice. "I can't talk about that."

"Let me come to see you."

"Not at my place."

"Tomorrow. I can come up tomorrow. You tell me where."

"Give me that cell phone number again." I pictured the phone cradled with her shoulder as she scribbled down the number. "What time would you get in the area?"

"You name it. Take me five hours to be in the District."

"No. Come about as far as one of the first rest stops outside the Beltway, in Virginia. No, better still, one of the restaurants just off 95, you know, one of those God-awful Virginia places like Wooden Bridge or something. Get there about ten or ten-thirty and wait for me to call you on your cell phone."

"It's Woodbridge. Jesus, Tracy, this sounds like, well, awfully cloak-and-dagger."

"Will you be there?"

"I'll be there."

A pause, and then with a tremor in her voice she said, "Weav?"

"Yeah?"

"Be prepared. I don't look so good."

Chapter Nine

I knew I had to tell Elly where I was going. I certainly owed her that. Before going, I really wanted to talk to my friend, SBI Agent Ballsford Twiddy. It would be good to have him on my side and filled-in on the situation before I got too mired in this mess. Sheriff Albright had said Balls was coming into town late today. I called the Sheriff's Department. Ethel answered when I got switched to Albright's office.

"No," she said, "Agent Twiddy called the sheriff and said he was still tied up and wouldn't be here until at least Wednesday." She puffed out a sigh. "They just don't let up on that poor man."

Then I telephoned Elly to see if she could go out to eat tonight, that I wanted to talk to her. I didn't want to go into too much detail at that time, but I did say I had to go up to the Washington area tomorrow.

"I thought you might," she said.

I couldn't tell anything by the tone of her voice, just a blankness as if she'd pulled down that familiar shade again over her emotions. Yet, I knew she must have felt natural twinges of uneasy jealousy when leftover ghosts of my life rattled out of the closet.

Because of her young son, Martin, Elly didn't like to go out often during the week, even though her mother was there to tend to him, so I wasn't surprised when she said maybe we'd better not try to go out to eat.

"I do want to talk with you a bit," I said.

"Go ahead. It's okay." Maybe she thought that sounded too abrupt. "Really," she said more softly, "I can talk."

That was a signal that she did have at least a degree of privacy. Still it was not as good as seeing her in person, being able to look right at her as I talked. Tell the truth, too, I just wanted to be near her.

I told her about the strange telephone conversations with Tracy Keller, and how she wanted to meet me on the Virginia side of the District, outside of town. "I know that, maybe, you don't feel all that comfortable about me going up there."

"I'm just worried about your getting so involved in this," she said. She gave a little mirthless laugh. "Like this past summer. You almost got us both killed." She referred to the murder of the young woman from the cast of *The Lost Colony*, the same case that Schweikert referred to. "I don't know what's going on, but something is, and I'm worried about you getting involved in it."

"Schweikert thinks I'm already involved."

We talked some more, and I promised her I was going to try to talk to Agent Ballsford Twiddy about what I was doing. That wasn't exactly a lie. But I felt bad about stretching the truth a bit. I was going to *try* to talk to him, but since he was still not here, I didn't know when I would talk with him, certainly not before I left by five or five-thirty in the morning.

She spoke softly, as I heard in the background her two co-workers chatting together as they came back in, "Harrison, please be careful. Please. And come back to me."

When I hung up the phone, I felt vaguely depressed. I didn't really want to be involved in this at all. For a few moments I even contemplated not going to the Washington area the next morning. But I knew I would, and I knew I would follow this through all the way. A failing of mine, perhaps, just the same that's the way I am.

I ate a light meal that night at home and went to bed early, but it didn't do any good. I had a lot of trouble going to sleep and then I woke up twice. I checked the clock at four-thirty, and went ahead and got up. Flipped the coffeemaker on in the kitchen and while I waited for it I stood at the sliding glass doors and looked outside at the darkness. I stepped out onto the porch. The wood felt cool and a little damp under my feet, but the air felt good, crisp and tinged with that sweet and salty, almost female, smell of the ocean. Stars were out, the half moon well over in the western sky toward the pine trees that silhouetted black against the sky. Just a few slips of clouds moved gray against the darker sky toward the south. I looked up at my windsock. Wind fairly light out of the north or north-east.

I got my coffee, took a shower, fixed a bowl of oatmeal in the microwave, and was ready to go by twenty after five. Cleared the answering machine, checked around upstairs. I put my camera bag on the floor in the back. I had my small Sony tape recorder and notepad, standard equipment. I felt a little foolish doing it, but I went back upstairs and got my S&W .32 revolver. I keep it wrapped in a slightly oily rag in the bottom drawer of my bedside table; I brought it down, holding it against my leg like I was hiding it from the darkness, and put it under the front seat in the car. In the utility room I keep paper towels and glass cleaner for the windshield. Mist and salt spray often come in during the night. I checked the oil, then let the car idle while I cleaned the windows. Even after all that, I was ready to pull out of the driveway by twenty of six. Over toward the beach the sky was getting lighter, paling out the stars.

Traffic was very light on the Bypass. I met a bread truck, Food Lion tractor-trailer and a few good old boys in pickups or older SUVs getting an early start on construction jobs. Two fishermen, with surfcasting rods affixed to the front bumper, scurried south like predatory beetles. I cracked the window slightly, and settled back as I drove, the tires on the Saab making a comfortable singing sound. I felt good, buoyed, like I always did at the beginning of a trip.

I just hoped I would feel this good at the end of the day.

During the season when I get north above Coinjock, I usually swing west on to US 158 and go by way of Camden Courthouse and South Mill, back on to 58, skirting the Great Dismal Swamp, and up through Suffolk to 460, hooking up with the Interstate loop around Richmond and on into Washington. But this time of year, with traffic lighter, I stayed straight toward Chesapeake and the Norfolk area, and took the relatively new bridge-tunnel over the James River at Newport News. Big Navy ships ghosted gray against the horizon on the right and freighters loaded with West Virginia coal on the left as I came up out of the tunnel at the end of the bridge.

I had my cell phone turned on the whole time, halfway expecting a call from Tracy saying she wouldn't make it. On 64 north of Williamsburg I pulled into the rest stop and carried my phone in my pocket to the restroom. Making excellent time.

No sooner had I settled back in the car than my cell phone gave its chirpy ring, like an insect. I rarely received incoming calls on it and the ring startled me.

It was Tracy. "Weav, where are you?"

I told her.

Static and traffic background noise distorted her voice. "Between ten and ten-thirty do you think you could be at the Manassas exit, Route 234?"

I glanced again at my watch. "Sure."

"There's a Cracker Barrel restaurant there." She chuckled. "Ought to be just the place for a Southern boy like you." Then the lightness was gone from her voice. "See you there." She clicked off.

I punched the accelerator. Most of the traffic sped along at seventy and above. I swung around the loop north of Richmond, then Fredericksburg and beyond. A few miles after I passed Quantico on I-95, I approached the Woodbridge-Manassas exit, Route 234. Be enough tourists, grandmas and kids at the Cracker Barrel that Tracy and I would be just two more travelers among the crowd.

I pulled into the parking lot right on the button of five after ten. Even past the usual morning breakfast hour, there were at least twenty-five cars in the lot. I pulled around to the far side of the parking lot, leaving several spaces between me and the next car. I backed into the space so I could see the front of the parking area and the drive anyone would use to get to the restaurant. I cut the engine and sat there holding the cell phone in my hand, wondering if she would really show up. Less than a minute later the phone rang.

I flipped open the phone.

Tracy chuckled a bit on the other end, sounding more like herself. "Feel more at home here at the Cracker Barrel?"

"What?" I looked around quickly, twisting in the seat, like maybe I would see her hiding under some bush.

"I just got here less than five minutes ago and I saw you drive in. I thought this would be a good place. I'm on the pay phone inside."

"I'll be right in."

"No, meet you on the front porch. Justa settin' on one of them thar rocking chers," faking a ridiculous Southern accent.

As I walked toward the front of the restaurant, with its faux rustic front and rocking chairs lined up on each side of the entrance, Tracy came out. She wore huge sunglasses, green cotton slacks, a tan windbreaker over a polo shirt. Her hair was a little longer than the last time I saw her and was brushed down over her ears rather than back like she used to wear it. Somehow it made her face look a little fatter, or puffy.

I grinned and she smiled back. As I stepped up on the porch I saw her face *was* puffy, and that the sunglasses were there to try to hide her eyes.

Someone had beat the hell out of her.

"Oh, Tracy," I said. I felt almost sick. I gave her a hug, kissed her lips lightly, off-center, in one of the two or three accepted Washington-style kisses, and then put my hand up gently to her face. As I did I touched her left ear, hidden under her hair. She flinched.

"Careful," she said and tried to make a little funny face, but it didn't quite work. I thought for a moment she would break down. "I told you I didn't look too good."

Make up, which she never wore that I remembered, had been applied to try to conceal a yellowish bruise on her chin and left cheek. Both eyes were swollen and the right one had blackened.

Then, through the strands of hair, I saw crusted blood and ointment on the top of her left ear, right where it joined her head. It was that same type of injury I had seen on Carter Lewiston, just not as severe.

My whole body felt cold. "What's his name?"

She fought for control. She nodded toward the chairs. We sat in the last two chairs on the parking lot side. An elderly woman came out and sat on the other side of the main entrance, her pocketbook on her lap, holding it with both hands, waiting for someone inside.

"I don't know his name."

"What?" I couldn't believe it.

"I really don't. He made sure of that."

"He was the one hired you to check on Carter Lewiston?"

She nodded.

"What in the hell were you doing passing yourself off as a private investigator?"

"You know me. Trying something new. I put an ad, practically a free one, in the Montgomery County paper, thinking I wouldn't get any response. If I did, I figured I'd give it a try and see whether I liked it and maybe, you know, get a license and all that."

I was shaking my head.

"Anyway, this guy contacted me. Called me. I met him at a restaurant in Wheaton, and he offered me five hundred dollars—in cash, ten fifty-dollar bills—to go to the Outer Banks to see what I could dig up on a man named Carter Lewiston."

"What were you supposed to find?"

"He said check on him at the courthouse, credit bureau, just keep asking around about him, and he said don't take no for an answer if people try to stonewall you. Let 'em know you mean business. He said Carter Lewiston was trying to weasel out of a business deal. I really went down there swaggering around, figured I was hot stuff."

"Yeah, I heard."

An elderly man came out of the restaurant and he and the woman walked slowly and gingerly off of the porch, headed toward the parking lot. The wind shifted and I could smell the cooking odors from the restaurant, like a mixture of bacon and vegetable soup.

"But, hell, Weav, here was a free trip to the Outer Banks, do a little digging. What harm, right?" Again, she looked as though the tears might come.

"He called Sunday late morning and said he wanted to come by and hear my report." She swallowed and I watched her throat. "I started to give him my address and he said he knew where I lived. I know I should have suspected something then. How did he know? Stupid, I realize, but I figured this was one slick guy and I kind of liked the, you know, B-grade movie thrill of it all. The mysterious stranger, giving out money."

She looked off toward the Interstate and its steady drone of traffic, trying to tell me the story as it happened.

"While I waited for him, I leafed through *The Washington Post*. Just glancing at headlines mostly. Then in the Metro Section or whatever they call it I saw a small item with the headlines *Outer Banks Radio Personality Slain*. The man killed was Carter Lewiston. I thought, Oh my God.

"My hands were shaking. I paced back and forth in the living room, and kept looking out the window. I didn't know what to think. Then his car drove up. A dark-colored Cadillac. He came walking up toward the house, looking cool and almost a smile on his face."

She gave a little shudder as memory of the moment crept across her. "When I let him in, he was as pleasant as could be, always that sort of half-smile on his face like he was really enjoying himself."

Tracy stopped talking as a young couple came from the parking lot, practically dragging a whining young girl by the hand, and crossed the porch in front of us to go into the restaurant.

Tracy gripped the arm of the rocking chair. Her fingers twitched. She said, "I told him the man I was investigating . . ." She gave a short laugh. "Yeah, investigating. Some investigation. I said the man had been killed.

"Then he did something that gave me the creeps. He put his hand against my cheek and said with a real syrupy Southern accent, 'Don't you worry your pretty little head about that, darlin'.' It was the way he touched me, and the look in his eyes.

They're blue but not like warm blue, more like, I don't know, the pigment ran out of them or something. All the while he's got that half-smile on his face."

I said, "I think I've seen him."

She looked startled, fear there on her face.

"On the beach at the Outer Banks—with Carter Lewiston," I said.

"Oh, God."

"He's the one who did all of this to you?" Of course I knew he was.

"He didn't need to. Didn't need to at all. I told him I wasn't going to say anything about investigating Carter Lewiston." She tightened her lips, then exhaled slowly through her nose. "He touched my face again. I backed up and he put his hand on the back of my neck, like pulling me toward him a little. He said, 'I know you're not going to say anything about it, darlin'. That's between you and me.' He kept calling me darlin' in that syrupy Southern accent. Then his smile was gone, just like that, and he hit me. His fist. He hit me in the stomach, really hard. I doubled up and he hit me in the face with his other hand. I went back over my coffee table, broke the legs on it. I tried to scramble away, but he grabbed my ankle and jerked me toward him."

She looked away from me and took a deep breath. I waited, my hand resting lightly on her wrist.

"He didn't have to keep hitting me." She turned toward me, her eyes narrowed with anger. "He was enjoying it. He had that smile back on his face. I fell down again and that's when he grabbed my ear and made me get on my knees, all the while twisting my ear. He stood real close. Had my face right up close to him, and I thought he was going to make me, you know, do something else.

"I was crying and begging him to stop. But I knew no one could hear me. You remember. My house. Off by itself."

Three people came out of the restaurant. The man was laughing and patting his stomach, a toothpick in the corner of his mouth.

When they were out of earshot, Tracy continued, "He slapped me across my face and told me to shut up. Then he leaned down, his face close to mine. He smelled like peppermint. He whispered, 'Forget you ever saw me.' Then he smiled real big, making me look at his face. 'You do want to keep on living, don't you, darlin'?' I tried to nod. He took his foot and pushed me over backwards."

She sat up straighter, her chin up, trying to look proud, as if she was in control. "He left. Closed the door quietly. I heard his car start, drive away."

I watched her throat as she swallowed. "And, Weav, I'm scared. That's not like me. But I'm scared."

"And you don't know his name? No phone number?"

She shook her head.

I gave her a quick version of my encounter at the beach, describing Mr. Charmer.

She gave a stiff and jerky nod of her head. "That's him, that's him."

"I think you should talk with the police. I've got a good friend with the North Carolina State Bureau. He'd be a good one, and he's going to be at the Outer Banks."

She thought a moment. "I don't really want to stay at my place."

"My place? Outer Banks? I owe you, remember."

She smiled at that, but was kind enough not to remind me of what a mess I had been. "Your place sounds good . . . long enough to talk to that friend of yours, the detective."

Despite myself, I thought about Elly, and how in the hell I would handle that. Well, I would just think about that later, like Scarlett O'Hara.

"I could get a few things. Drive down today even, or early tomorrow morning. Let me think about it," she said. Then she sat straighter in the rocking chair, held her shoulders back. "Want to go inside get some grits and biscuits?"

The women I know have such good appetites. "Sure."

"Nobody knows us here. They'll just think you've been beating me up again."

A young hostess, looking very officious, led us to a booth. She put down the menus and said flatly, "Enjoy your meal."

We glanced at the menus. Tracy put hers down. "Two eggs over light, sausage, toast, coffee and orange juice."

"Sounds good to me," I said, as a rather tired looking waitress came to our booth. As she wrote down our orders, I saw her glance at Tracy.

Then the old Tracy I knew just had to surface. With a barely concealed smile that disappeared as quickly as a blink of the eye, she practically sobbed, "You promised you wouldn't do that anymore."

The waitress glared at me, snatched the menus I held toward her, made a little "hurumpf" sound in her throat, and left.

"Thanks a lot," Tracy.

That grin of hers was there.

But Tracy didn't leave it at that. She was having too much fun. When the waitress brought our food, and plopped my plate in front of me, Tracy said with a break in her voice, as if she were just finishing a conversation, ". . . and you told me you weren't going to see her anymore."

I got another glare from the waitress that would have seared the hide off a mule.

Tracy chuckled quietly as she buttered her toast and got ready to devour her eggs.

We went over the plans once again. Tracy would go straight up toward the Pentagon, then swing over to the George Washington Parkway, back up around the Beltway to her place in Maryland, get a few things and then drive down to the Outer Banks late that afternoon. She would call me just before she got to the Wright Memorial Bridge over Currituck Sound, and I would meet her and lead her to my place. But after we finished eating, she said she had suddenly gotten tired, and didn't feel like driving all the way down there today. The skin around her cheeks, despite the make-up, looked stretched and almost translucent. I knew she had slept very little. She said she would, instead, rest this afternoon and night and get a very early start in the morning.

Frankly, I was relieved because that would give me more time to visit with Elly and explain the situation. Also, if Tracy came earlier in the day, we might find her another place to stay. Arriving late at night, I wouldn't want to shuffle her off some place. But it made me feel wimpy as hell that I was thinking like that, as if I weren't my own man or something.

I left the waitress a sizable tip, hoping I guess that it would redeem me somewhat in her eyes.

Outside, I gave Tracy a hug and a light kiss on her lips. We parted and I stood there as she walked across the parking lot, her shoulders held proudly. I watched her get into her seven-year-old dusty Toyota, and drive off, waving one hand as she did. But she suddenly looked somehow small and vulnerable sitting in that car by herself, wearing those big sunglasses, trying to smile.

Maybe it would have been different if I had insisted she come down that same afternoon, or if I had gone up to Maryland with her while she got few belongings.

That became another thing that haunts me, another ghost in my life.

Chapter Ten

Before leaving the Cracker Barrel, I went back inside to use the restroom. As I came out and past the motherly looking woman serving as cashier, she smiled and said, "Have a nice day." I nodded, and she said, "And don't frown so much, young man."

"Yeah," I mumbled and did a fair job of smiling back at her.

But I knew the frown was there again as I got in the car and maneuvered from 134 to the exit heading south on I-95. I accelerated into the southbound traffic, eased over a lane, driving mechanically because my mind was on Tracy, and that son-of-a-bitch Mr. Charmer, on the slaying of Carter Lewiston, and what in the devil it all meant. Thoughts bounced around. There was also the business of Rick Schweikert wanting to pin Lewiston's death on me.

I had to clear my thinking, devise a plan, take it step by step.

First, I knew I had to get in touch with Agent Twiddy. I needed to see if he could meet with me and Tracy when she came down tomorrow. I knew he would believe me and certainly believe Tracy after he took one look at her. Schweikert's opinion didn't particularly bother me. He couldn't honestly entertain the thought that I had killed Carter Lewiston. Schweikert hated my guts but he wasn't totally stupid. That didn't mean he wouldn't try to hassle me on the slaying, give me a hard time with threats. But accuse me of murder? That was a little farfetched . . . I hoped.

But the big question was still: What does it all mean? Why would anyone do a professional execution-style assassination of Carter Lewiston? Do this after beating him up and ripping his ear. The most controversial thing Carter Lewiston had ever done, that I knew of, was to play a selection of Mahler rather than Mozart on his Sunday morning classical radio program. I was convinced the killing was done by that same guy, and the same one who hired Tracy and then, for no apparent reason and with evil enjoyment, used his fists and his foot on her, twisting her ear the same way.

I was hardly aware of driving. The miles sped by. I thought about making a restroom stop, but drove on past a rest stop on I-64 because I was in the left lane, speeding along. I realized I was pushing a bit over eighty and eased off a tad. Checked the gas gauge, and figured I could make it to Southland at the North Carolina line. I had been driving less than four hours, making excellent time when I pulled in at Southland and gassed up. I decided I might as well get a very late lunch or early dinner at the restaurant. I ordered the vegetable plate, including the specialty of fried okra. I nursed a cup of coffee that was too weak. I was staring off into space when I realized the waitress had said something to me. "I'm sorry, what? Dessert? No. No, thanks. Check please." I paid and over-tipped her. But I believe in that, no matter what. Outside I stretched and arched my back. Only then did I realize how tired I was. Glanced at my watch. About another fifty minutes to go, sticking to the speed limit—more or less.

Crossing over the Wright Memorial Bridge I glanced at the waters of the Currituck Sound automatically to check whether the boating conditions were favorable. Waves only about one foot. Maybe tomorrow. No, I knew there was no way. Halfway across I glanced at the sign that said "Dare County." Always felt at home when I saw that.

I pulled off the Bypass onto Fourth Street and then to my little house on a cul-de-sac. The first thing I did when I got in the house—after speaking to my parakeet and stepping over the bass—was to place another call to Agent Twiddy. Had to leave a message, asking him to call me.

Then I took a deep breath and sat in the chair by the phone, mentally composing my report to Elly and the fact that Tracy was coming down, and how she had been beaten up. I took another deep breath, glanced at my watch, and dialed Elly at home. She had just gotten in.

"Oh, I'm so glad you're back safely. I've been hoping I would hear from you all day." She sounded rather breathless. She paused a beat. "How did it go? You saw . . . saw that woman?"

"She'd been beat up."

"What?"

"Beat up. Her face was . . . was, well, beat up."

"Oh, my lord. Who?"

"The man who hired her to do that, that, stupid so-called investigation of Carter Lewiston."

"Oh, Harrison. I don't like this." I sensed that she had sat on the sofa. "What have you gotten yourself into?"

"He has to be the same one I saw on the beach with Lewiston. Has to be."

"Please, please don't get anymore involved. Let the sheriff handle this, or your friend Agent Twiddy. Don't you do it."

"Well. . . ."

"Do you hear me, Harrison? Let it go. Please."

"Well, Elly, she's coming down tomorrow to talk with Agent Twiddy and probably the sheriff."

Her voice rose: "Coming down here?"

"Elly, there's a connection. She's the key. She doesn't know the man's name but she can describe him. Maybe with one of the artist from Raleigh we can get a sketch and—"

"You don't have any business getting involved in this."

"I'm already involved."

There was a pause on the line. I could hear her breathing. "Why did he beat her up?"

"Two reasons, the best I can figure. One, because she knows what he looks like, and two, he's just plain mean. He enjoys hurting people."

"Harrison?"

"Yes?"

"He knows you know what he looks like too."

We talked a bit more and I tried to assure her I would be all right. She didn't really buy it. I'm not sure I did either.

That night I slept more soundly than I thought I would. The next morning I had just fixed coffee and started out on the deck to drink it—feeling pretty good, despite all that was going on—when the phone rang.

I figured it had to be Agent Twiddy.

"Hello."

"Harrison? Harrison Weaver?"

I didn't recognize the woman's voice. She sounded like she might be choking back a sob. "Yes?" I realized dread was growing in my stomach. "This is Harrison Weaver."

"This is Jean Clayborne."

The sense of dread grew. Jean worked with Tracy Keller at Hand Gun Restriction. The dread mushroomed, a palatable weight in my gut.

"You probably don't know, and I hate, I hate to tell you like this, but—"

"Tell me." I hated what I was almost certain she would say.

"Tracy. Tracy was killed yesterday. Someone ran her off the GW Parkway . . . into the ravine. A hit-and-run."

I sat down suddenly, holding the phone so tightly my hand began to cramp. I don't remember exactly what I said next except that I kept muttering that often-used expletive over and over.

Then I came back around. "Any details at all that you have, Jean?"

She told me what little she had learned late last night from other friends and on the evening news. Newscasters cautiously reported her compact car had been sideswiped by a large SUV. They stopped short of saying the SUV forced the smaller car into the ravine near one of the overlooks, a drop of several hundred feet toward the Potomac River. But a driver who was some distance behind the two vehicles said it looked to him as if the SUV deliberately rammed Tracy's car, then sped off. When Park Police and medics got down the ravine to Tracy's car, they tried to revive her, but apparently she was already dead, even though the reports were unclear whether she died on impact or was pronounced dead at the hospital, Jean said.

"Not that it makes any difference at this point," she sobbed.

Before we hung up, Jean promised she would call me with information on funeral or memorial services as soon as she heard. I took down her number.

I sat there hunched over without moving for quite some time. I felt sick, almost as if I might throw up. My eyes welled with tears, tears of sadness, frustration, and anger. My breathing was rapid and shallow.

I realized I mumbled aloud, "Oh, Tracy, poor Tracy." I lurched from the chair and stumbled to the kitchen sink. I bent over the basin, propping myself up on my forearms. I heaved but nothing came up. I kept shaking my head and tears veiled my eyes. I splashed water on my face.

Still numb, but forcing myself to function, I dabbed at my face with a paper towel and went back to the table by the phone. I flipped on my electronic address book for the direct line to one of two detectives with Arlington County I had worked with on a magazine article a few months earlier. We had become friends, as was often the case in doing the research on a murder story, and I believed he would do me a favor, even though Tracy's killing—and I wasn't about to believe it was simply a hit-and-run—technically was under the jurisdiction of the National Park Police. I rubbed my eyes with the crumbled paper towel so I could read the number that came on the little screen.

I was surprised that Detective Dwight McAlister answered on the first ring. After brief greetings, for he knew I wasn't calling to chitchat, I told him I was trying to find out more about the death of my friend, Tracy Keller, on the GW Parkway yesterday.

There was a pause. Then he said, "Give me your number. I'll make a couple of calls, get back with you. Won't take long."

My coffee was not only cold but tasted old. I dumped it in the sink and made another small pot. I had given up smoking cigarettes years earlier, but I started playing with cigars a few months back. I suddenly wanted one, and took one from a make-shift humidor I had created, and went out on the porch with it along with my fresh coffee. I moved like a zombie. I sat in one of the web-backed chairs. I stared off over the tops of the pine trees. With the back of my hand that smelled of the cigar, I wiped away a tear from my cheek.

I know, as well as anyone, the futility of "what if," but just the same I kept replaying the thought that if only Tracy had come straight down to North Carolina with me. Then, again, when did the hit-and-run driver start tailing her. I knew she was targeted. She had to be. Was he there at the Cracker Barrel, watching all the time?

If so. . . . A chill came over me.

I picked up my coffee cup. Cold again and the cigar had gone out.

The phone rang. I glanced at my watch. Ten-twenty.

"It's McAlister," he said, his accent clipped, carrying traces of early years in Chicago. "I got something from a friend with Fairfax PD. The vehicle believed involved in the hit-and-run was stolen yesterday A.M. Late model Range Rover. Recovered early morning today in a parking area at Tyson's Corner. Damage to the right side consistent with the victim's Toyota."

He paused. "You owe me," he said.

"Yeah. I sure appreciated it, Dwight."

"There's something else," he said. "That wasn't just a plain hit-and-run."

I braced myself. "Yeah?"

"There was a bullet hole in the door on the driver's side. The window was down." I knew he had something else to say, and I dreaded it. "There was another bullet—this one on the front left side of the victim's forehead, as if maybe she'd turned to look at the other vehicle and her assailant. Small caliber. Probably a .22. She was banged up pretty bad and the medics might not have even noticed when they extricated her from the vehicle."

I know he could hear me breathing. His voice softened. "This a real close friend of yours?"

"A good friend. I just saw her yesterday. Yesterday morning in Virginia. She was supposed to be on her way home in Maryland."

There was another pause on his end, waiting for me to say more. When I didn't speak, he said, "You in trouble?"

"I don't know."

"You don't think this was, say, road rage?"

"Do you?"

"Probably not. Neither does my colleague with Fairfax."

I figured I needed to tell him something more. "A guy had beat her up. That's the reason she was in Virginia to talk to me. I think he targeted her."

"You know who he is?"

"No. Wish I did, I'd go after the son of a bitch."

"Hey, Weaver, no Lone Ranger shit, okay? I think maybe you better talk to somebody."

"Yeah, well I am. I've got an appointment this morning with a good friend, an agent with the North Carolina SBI." A small lie, but I was hoping to have an appointment with him today.

I could hear him tapping a pencil on his desk, other squad room noise in the background. "You know, Weaver, this perp just might not be satisfied with getting the woman. He might be thinking about doing a number on one of her 'real good friends,' if you get my drift."

"I'm way down in North Carolina. Outer Banks."

"Yeah, but don't that highway run both ways? Just don't be driving near no ravines." He muttered "shit" under his breath. "Forget I said that. Nothing to be funny about."

There was nothing funny running through my mind. Just like Elly said, I was convinced Tracy was killed at least partly because this guy appeared to take pleasure in doing harm—and the bigger part of it was that she could identify him as the one who hired her to investigate Carter Lewiston and then viciously beat her up.

Playing not far in the back of my mind, too, was the other fact Elly had mentioned—that I could identify him as the one who was with Carter Lewiston at the beach that day.

Chapter Eleven

I needed to call Elly at the Register of Deeds. I was glad Elly answered rather than one of the other two women.

I said, "I know this isn't a good time, calling at the office, but a lot has happened." I knew she could tell by my tone that this wasn't just a casual call.

"Go ahead," she said, a touch of distance in her voice.

"Tracy Keller was killed right after I left. Someone forced her car off the road, down a ravine at the Potomac."

"No . . . oh, my God." Her voice was whispery.

"That's not all of it." She waited. I knew she could hear me take a breath. "She had a bullet in her head."

"Harrison!" Her voice was an urgent, hoarse whisper. I could almost see her gripping the phone, standing rigidly at her desk, stepping away a few feet and with her back to the other women in her office. "What have you got yourself into? Get away from those people. Stay away!"

I wanted to say, "What people?" The only persons I knew of linked to that guy were now dead—except me. But I said nothing for a moment. I knew she was waiting. "The guy who beat her up—the one who hired her to do that phony investigation of Carter Lewiston—is the one who shot her, ran her off the road in a stolen SUV. Killed her."

"Same one . . ." She lowered her voice even more, ". . . who did that to Mr. Lewiston?"

"I'm convinced."

"Oh, Harrison, what do you do now? Please, please leave this alone."

"I'm trying to get in touch with Agent Twiddy."

"Do it right away."

"I'm trying."

Her voice took on a different tone, trying to sound more casual but still talking softly. "Be careful. This isn't looking good."

"I know."

When I hung up, I stood there looking at the phone. I was about to call the sheriff's office again to see if anyone knew of Agent Twiddy's whereabouts. Today it seemed providential: Every time I thought about the phone it rang.

When I picked it up, the husky male voice said, "Looks like soon as I get outta town you get yourself in trouble. Just left your buddy Rick Schweikert and he's hot to give you a hard time."

"Hello, Balls. So good of you to exchange pleasantries with me. But to tell the truth, I really don't feel so friggin' pleasant."

He must have sensed something in my voice because he waited a beat or two. "Yeah?"

I gave him a rapid rundown of what had happened in the Washington area to Tracy Keller. He knew all about Carter Lewiston and what I had told Sheriff Albright and Schweikert about seeing Mr. Charmer with Lewiston.

When I finished, my sentences running one into the other, I took a deep breath.

Balls said, "We better get together."

"When?"

"Now. I'm leaving Manteo in five. Meet me at Basnight's Lone Cedar restaurant."

I looked in the bathroom mirror and splashed more water on my face, then hurried out of the house. I knew Balls would be waiting for me when I got there, even pushing it as quickly as I could. It seemed I was always meeting Balls where there was food. We went back many years when I was with a newspaper and just getting started with the crime writing. Twenty-four minutes after Balls and I talked, I pulled in at the Lone Cedar, overlooking the water at the causeway to Roanoke Island and Manteo.

I found Balls right away, sitting apart from others at a booth. The early lunch crowd had already begun to arrive. His grin and moustache made him look like a husky Tom Selleck, the actor. He didn't get up but we shook hands. He had coffee and the remains of a few boiled shrimp. I signaled for a coffee.

The grin faded. "Okay, tell me about this mysterious stranger—the one only you have seen, according to Schweikert."

"My friend Tracy Keller saw him. One time too many."

"How do you know it was the same guy?"

"Ah, come on, Balls. He hires Tracy to stir up info on Carter Lewiston. I see Carter and this guy on the beach. Then Carter ends up dead—and so does Tracy. After he beats her up. And her description of him fits mine."

Balls nodded. He checked his plate in case he'd missed one of the shrimp. The young waitress brought my coffee. I said yes to her suggestion for shrimp, and another order for Balls.

Balls leaned back and spoke softly so I had to strain to hear. "Okay, he does a number on your friend. That's because she can identify him, even if she doesn't know his name. But the puzzle is, why the professional job on Carter Lewiston?"

"That's what I can't understand. Was Carter mixed up in something? Doesn't seem likely."

The waitress brought the shrimp, cocktail sauce, and crackers.

Balls went for the shrimp, plopped one in his mouth. "I'm checking Mr. Lewiston out. Never can tell."

We continued eating in silence for a few moments, then Balls wiped his mouth and said, "Two things come to mind. First of all, the mystery man is probably a freelance, working for someone else. A hired gun. That's my theory du jour." He got another shrimp.

"And the second thing?"

"Your ass might be right in this guy's gun-sight."

"Yeah, thanks for reminding me. I hadn't thought about it for four or five minutes."

"If he killed your friend because she could identify him, he knows you can ID him too. He had to be stalking her that morning she met you. He saw the two of you together. And he was probably the one you ran into at the beach with Lewiston." He looked at me, a dead-serious expression on his face. "The fact that the two of you—the Keller woman and you—went your separate ways that morning may have saved your life. He had to target one of you. He chose her . . . to start with."

"I don't want any more of the shrimp," I said.

"No sense in letting 'em go to waste," Balls said, giving me that Tom Selleck grin.

Then he got serious again. "I don't want to see you get yourself hurt. This guy—and I'm like you, I think it's the same guy did Lewiston and your friend—is deadly. And he's slick. He could be up on you before you know it."

I nodded. I knew damn well it was the truth.

"At the same time," Balls said, "maybe he figures you're enough removed from his . . . his activities, that you're not really a threat. Let's hope that's the case." Then the grin came back. "Heck, I don't want anything to happen to my Lucky Crime Solver."

Over the years I had been fortunate in stumbling across a clue, or even occasionally fitting together a puzzler of a crime, that had helped Balls in his work. In return, he'd gotten so he trusted me to keep my mouth shut when I should—put my pen away when necessary—and in turn he'd let me tag along with him as he worked a case, or at least keep me filled in on the progress, as long as my presence didn't compromise his work in any way. He was a proud professional and one hell of a good investigator.

I signaled the waitress, and got out my wallet. "Business expense," I said to Balls.

As we got to the front, Balls nodded toward my car. "Still driving that Snob, I see."

"A Saab, Balls."

"Oh, yeah."

"And I noticed when I drove up that you're sticking with that souped-up, vintage Thunderbird." It was pointed nose out, as was his usual style.

"A classic, my man, a classic."

The sky was blue, a light breeze out of the southwest. Temperature had to be low-seventies. Beautiful day.

I said, "I'm heading on back to the house—by way of paying my respects to the ocean."

"Keep your eyes open."

"I will."

He poked vigorously at his teeth with a toothpick he picked up on the way out. "First, I'm going to stop by the radio station and pay my condolences . . . and try to find out what sort of on-the-side business ventures Lewiston might have been involved in." He snapped the toothpick in half and tossed it. "Then I'm going by the sheriff's office, see if I can't manage to run into your buddy Schweikert, try to get him set straight."

"Good luck."

"But let's face it. Here you go see a friend and she ends up dead. Schweikert's going to play that for all it's worth. And, my little man, there's no way right now that you can prove you had nothing to do with it. Huh?"

"That's bullshit and you know it."

"Don't lose your cool. I know it. But it's the kind of thing Schweikert will play on."

I shook my head. I didn't feel I had time or inclination to be concerned with that pompous ass Schweikert.

Balls started toward his car, stopped and looked back with that shit-eating grin on his face. "Not going to swing by the courthouse to see that Pedersen gal?"

"Later," I said, "after you get Schweikert off my back. Elly doesn't need a 'prime suspect' hanging around her office."

He saw the look that had come over my face, and he took a step back toward me. "I'm sorry about your friend."

I nodded, the sadness washing over me again. So I turned and went to my car. I heard him say, "We'll get the bastard."

I vowed to myself that I'd personally get him.

Chapter Twelve

I took the Beach Road. The proper name is Virginia Dare Trail. Beach Road is what most of us call it. It's Highway 12. Runs north and south, the Bypass on the left as you head north and the Atlantic on the right. At several places you can still see the ocean. But with the building that has gone on in the past few years and the protective sand dunes that have been pushed into place to try vainly to keep the ocean at bay, the ocean is much less visible than it used to be. When I got up to Kill Devil Hills, I pulled once again into the parking area at the bathhouse and walkway to the beach.

I know my fascination with the ocean may sound a little corny, but maybe it's part of that feeling that we all came from the sea, or maybe it's being so close to something as powerful as the sea. Today, with a breeze out of the southwest, the tide ebbing, the ocean was flattened out with breakers low and tame as they pulsated against the brown sand. An elderly couple walked slowly south along the beach. No one else was around.

I breathed in deeply. Then turned, feeling strangely refreshed, and went to my car. But the peaceful feeling didn't last. The sadness over Tracy came back. I started the engine and revved it more than I needed to.

When I got to my house, I decided to use a ploy I've engaged in before to get my mind settled down. I would practice the bass. Play scales if nothing else. Warm enough, too, that I could put Janey's cage out on the deck for a while after I got through practicing.

Using the electronic tuner, I brought the A string into pitch. Then tuned the other three strings using harmonics. Helped with ear training, I figured. As soon as the bass sounded, Janey began to chirp happily.

I had just finished a good solid ten minutes of playing—but avoiding the Mozart piece—when Jean called from Hand Gun Restriction with details of the memorial service for Tracy Keller.

The service was to be held next Wednesday at eleven A.M. at a small Presbyterian church in Arlington.

Since Tracy didn't have a church she attended, one of her friends at Hand Gun Restriction had arranged with her minister to conduct the services at his church. Tracy's brother and step-mother both agreed that Tracy had said that when her time came she wanted to be cremated, her ashes scattered along a favorite nature trail of hers in Maryland.

"I will be at the service," I said. "No, I won't try to speak. There'll be plenty of others who will"

In order to try to stop thinking about Tracy and the murder of Lewiston, I called Elly to see if we couldn't get together that night.

She paused, then said, "Why don't you come over here for a light supper? Good country ham biscuits, Mother said. Salad, applesauce."

"Sounds great. Can I bring something?"

"Just yourself. Safely." She spoke softly. "Anything else happen?"

"No, other than meeting with Agent Twiddy."

"I caught a glimpse of him leaving the radio station and then coming into the courthouse."

"I think he was going to try to calm Schweikert down."

"Good luck," she said.

Then I took a deep breath and told her about the memorial service.

"You're going, I suppose? I'll worry about that, your safety."

"Be a lot of folks around."

Again, there was a pause. "Harrison?"

"Yes?"

"Maybe we can talk a bit tonight."

After we hung up, I didn't feel so good. Anytime a woman says something about "needing to talk," it puts a damper on a man's spirits. I'm no exception. Just the vaguest trace of distancing in her voice, and I knew there was something bothering Elly, something she needed to vent. I figured I knew what it was. She had a degree of peacefulness in her life before she met me. She had about recovered from the death of her young husband; she was living there comfortably with her mother and her son Martin; she had a job she liked at the Register of Deeds; and then I arrived on the scene. She was almost "collateral damage" in the earlier murder investigation I was involved in, and now she sees me getting deeply mired in this latest. I didn't want to be a disruptive force in her life. I moved here seeking the same serene life she was leading. Yet, here I was again with murder and mayhem swirling about me.

I sat in the chair by the phone for a few moments. Then I forced myself to get up, get busy. I knew I needed to at least try to get work done on a true-crime book that was under contract. I was more than half through it and had done stacks of research and interviews during the winter. The book dealt with a woman, finally arrested in a small Piedmont North Carolina city after she had poisoned three husbands, and was working on the fourth. Well, I was ahead of deadline. I wrote a bit, sighed, pushed back from the computer.

I couldn't get Tracy's death and that of Carter Lewiston's off my mind, and I guess I had a vague sense of unease about Elly's wanting to talk. Then, as the thoughts of the two slayings bounced around in my head, a similarity suddenly occurred to me.

In both killings, there had been preliminary build-up. The killer had punched Lewiston while they were on the beach, and torn his ear. Then later, two days later, he kills him.

The same with Tracy. Beat her up first. Even did the ear thing. Then a couple of days later he kills her.

In both instances there was the—God, what was it? Foreplay?—before the actual killing.

That evil son of a bitch enjoyed tormenting and then killing. I was convinced of that.

Elly lives on a dead-end road near the Manteo Airport. I got there right at six, dressed Outer Banks style in khaki slacks, cotton golf shirt, a pair of L.L. Bean beach shoes, a type of sneaker with mesh tops and drain holes in the soles so water can run through.

As usual, when I drove up to their somewhat secluded white frame house, similar to one of the Sears ready-to-build packages that were sold nationwide in the 1930s, Elly came onto the porch, held up her hand and wiggled her fingers in greeting. Little Martin stood slightly behind his mother, un-smiling, holding on tightly to the leg of her white slacks. He did nod at me when I stepped up onto the low porch and greeted him.

Elly had her hair tied up in the back, and I always like that because it shows off her neck and looks appealing the way a little bit of the hair works loose, brushing her neck.

She looks delicate, with her fair skin and dark hair, but she is the first to announce that she's a tough "Outer Banks gal," and that's no idle boast.

She has lived here all of her life except for a few years in Raleigh. She and her young husband had lived in Raleigh where he performed with the North Carolina Symphony, a cellist. She had met him when she was enrolled at Meredith College. His health was never good, and he died quite suddenly of an especially virulent strain of pneumonia that doctors at first thought was just a bad case of flu. Elly and I shared common sorrows. We had both lost spouses.

We went inside and I could smell the pleasant aroma of the country ham and hot biscuits. I took a deep breath.

"Simple supper, Harrison," Elly said.

I glanced at a newspaper page on the end table by the sofa. The page was folded to the crossword puzzle. Elly, who her friend Linda Shackleford said was addicted to crossword puzzles, had filled in most of the puzzle—with a ballpoint pen. "See you've about finished it," I said, nodding at the crossword.

"Stuck on a couple of them. Could look it up, I guess, but I'd rather think about. Sometimes they come to you."

"See you've got one of your history books there, too."

Elly laughed. "Yes, Linda's always teasing me that I talk about the Punic Wars. Thought I'd read up on them again and really wow her."

Elly had majored in history—and maybe crossword puzzles—at Meredith College.

Mrs. Pedersen, Elly's mother, came into the living room. "Supper's ready if you all are," she said, smiling. She is taller than Elly, erect, with short thick gray hair. Elly takes more after her late father, a transplanted Dane from Minnesota, who came to the Outer Banks with the Coast Guard, met the woman who was to become Elly's mother and never left.

For me, the supper was anything but simple. Homemade hot biscuits with country ham that wasn't overcooked, sliced tomatoes and cucumbers with a splash of vinegar, salt and pepper and sugar, stewed corn, a bowl of Mrs. Pedersen's homemade applesauce, and for me, a small dish of steamed okra.

"You want some of my okra, Martin?"

He ignored me.

"Say no thank you, Martin."

I said, "He spoke to me the other day. Didn't you, Martin?"

He eyed me seriously, but then a trace of a smile began to creep across his face.

After we ate, Mrs. Pedersen took Martin into the adjoining room to watch television while she did the dishes—alone, at her command. The evening was warm enough that Elly and I went out on the porch and sat on the two-person wooden swing suspended by chains from the ceiling. There in the growing darkness, the setting was like being back in another generation or two.

"Okay, Harrison, I have something to say."

"Uh-oh."

"Nothing bad. Well, bad in that I feel that way. About your friend, Ms. Keller. I feel bad that I got so upset with her, and then she got . . . got killed."

"Nothing you could have done differently. She was there to create a ruckus. She thought that was her job."

Elly was quiet a moment. Then, "And that's not all."

I looked at her. Another shoe about to drop?

"I worry about you," she said.

"I know."

"Really. Wives . . . well, wives and friends, and, you know, special friends, worry about their men who go out the Inlet as commercial fishermen, scallop boats, and all, because it can be dangerous. Very dangerous. But goodness sakes, Harrison, you're a writer and it's not supposed to be dangerous but you're always getting into danger. And . . . and well, I worry."

I took her hand. "That's sweet, Elly. But you really don't need to worry." Truthfully, I didn't feel that confident, and I'm sure that Elly knew me well enough to sense how I really felt.

She is "my girl," as we say here. And maybe we're both a lot more old-fashion than we admit. Not like in the movies, we didn't fall into bed upon making initial eye contact. No obligatory sex scene in this script of ours. Oh, we'd kissed passionately and were quickly approaching that point of no return—when, damnit, something always interrupted us, from a phone call, to Martin crying out in his sleep, or something. It had become a joke with us. But I figured, one of these days. . . .

Elly gave a short chuckle. "Maybe if you wrote true romance stories?"

"I haven't had enough experience."

"You're sure getting enough experience writing about violence."

"Strange because I'm not a violent type."

"Yeah, right," she said. "Just a shy, sensitive, retiring type."

There was a moment or two of silence while I sensed something else bubbled just under the surface. "Was there anything else, Elly? Anything else you wanted to talk about?"

She had gazed out over the yard to the tall pine trees that gave way to a thicker undergrowth. She turned toward me, then studied her hands folded in her lap. She gave a short little laugh. "It doesn't seem so . . . so important, so urgent now." The smile was back. "Once you are here with me, all of my fine speeches I thought I would make sort of fizzle out."

I waited, watching her face and her eyes.

She held her head to one side, concentrating, the hint of creases between her eyebrows. "Every now and then, Harrison, I get afraid. Afraid something will happen to you, and then—I know this sounds selfish—then I will go through that loss again. It's almost like I'm afraid something will happen and then you won't be there, and I'll be all alone again. . . . Oh, I know this doesn't make much sense."

I put my hand on her wrist. I wasn't sure what to say, so for one of those rare times I kept quiet, let her go on.

She gave that tiny laugh again. "I told you I had a speech that fizzled all out." The two lines were back between her eyebrows again. "I guess, like I've said before, sometimes I'm just afraid of feeling too much."

Then I spoke. "We're going slow, Elly. We're taking our time. Let's just enjoy." I figured a bit of bravado would help. "Besides, nothing's going to happen."

"You're kind of special to me, Harrison."

I thought for a moment a tear glistened in her eye. We had avoided using the "love" word. That time was fast approaching, though, I knew.

Just then Mrs. Pedersen came to the screen door. "I'll start getting Martin ready for bed," she said.

"I'll be in, Mother, in just a few minutes." To me, she said, "I guess I'd better. . . ."

"I know." I stepped just inside the living room and called out my thanks again to Mrs. Pedersen. Elly came in behind me. In the shadow away from the front door. I kissed her and felt her up against me close and I knew she could feel me, too. "One of these days, Miss Elly. One of these days."

She touched my lips with her fingertips. "I know," she said.

As I started to my car she said, "Harrison, please be careful." Then, to please me, she spoke with an exaggerated Outer Banks accent as she added, "It's high tide, you know, and the sea can get rough."

Traffic was extremely light as I drove east into Manteo. In my mind, I replayed some of the conversation we had just had. Remembrance of it left me vaguely depressed. I know she worried about getting too close, and we were getting really close. At times, as she said, she wanted to hold back, and then when we were together, that distancing tended to vanish. If I was honest with myself, as I am from time to time, I would admit that I, too, had concerns about getting too close, being hurt again. I guess we both were being cautious—when we weren't together.

The traffic light was going red as I approached the corner by Ace Hardware. I stopped, automatically checking the rear-view mirror. Nothing behind me. But suddenly, partially hidden beside the store, a dark-colored late model Cadillac pulled out, tires protesting as it swung sharply to the left, cutting in front of me and heading back in the direction I had come.

The driver sped by. I couldn't see his face clearly in that instant, but I could swear it was that son of a bitch. My heart beat faster. First impulse was to screw the red light and do a U-turn after him. But two cars came out of the other side street and got in my way. And what was I going to do? Make a citizen's arrest? On what grounds? I looked in the mirror again. He was gone. Turned up into one of the streets toward the center of Manteo.

Just the same, when the light changed I turned left instead of going straight and crept along toward the center of Manteo, keeping watch on all of the side streets I passed. Nothing. Hardly any traffic at all. I flipped open my cell phone and called Elly.

I told her to make sure she locked the door and to call the sheriff's office if a strange car showed up.

"It's probably nothing, Elly," I said, trying to make my voice sound calm, "and I most likely am just imagining things, but just the same . . . rough seas and all that, you know. Doesn't hurt to be extra careful."

"Harrison?"

"Yes?"

"Think about becoming a true romance writer."

In spite of the tension I felt, I had to chuckle. I went down Sir Walter Raleigh Street, took a side street across Budleigh, and drove back toward 64. No Cadillac.

Then I called Balls on his cell phone. I told him what I thought I had seen. He was quiet a moment. Then he said, "You still got that little peashooter of a handgun?"

"Yeah."

"Probably an illegal piece, but keep it with you. Get home. Don't be chasing around looking for some guy who may just be some old fart in his Cadillac tooling around. But lock up good when you get there—and call me again as soon as you get settled in."

As I headed east on the highway, I said to Balls, "I've got a feeling he may just be beginning to play with me. Keep me on edge. I think he's one evil son of a bitch, and he gets a kick out of this. His idea of foreplay."

Chapter Thirteen

When I got to my house, with nothing suspicious along the way, I left the carport light on and went inside and locked up good. Out of a bottom drawer I got my old short-barrel .32 caliber revolver, loaded it from the half-empty box of ammo. It had been years since I fired the thing, and then it was just target practice. I'd never shot it at another human being. No question, though, I'd kill that guy if he came after me. At least I think I would. Sure. I'd have to. Just the same, the thought of actually doing it gave me a chill.

I closed the blinds and drapes tightly. I picked up the bass, tightened the bow and rosined it, played a B-flat major scale, two octaves. The high B-flat was off. I tried it again. Same thing. "Shit," Janey said, bobbing her head and watching.

"Yeah, you said it for me," I said.

Next time I got it right.

Later on, when I went to bed, I slept soundly. Woke the next morning to bright sunshine. Maybe that wasn't the guy, anyway. I could be imagining things. I was determined to stick to my work, make progress on the book about the murderess, who if she hadn't tried to do in husband number four, probably would have gotten away with the triple homicides.

On Friday morning Balls called me. "Come on down to the courthouse, meet with me and Schweikert. Put his phony theory to rest."

By 9:45 I'd parked around the corner from the courthouse in front of Manteo Booksellers. I glanced in at the Register of Deeds office but Elly was busy working on something at her desk and didn't see me at first. Then she glanced up, sensing a presence. She smiled and I said I was going upstairs, and would see her shortly if she had a moment.

"Of course," she said. The other two women in the office gave each other knowing looks.

I met with Balls in a small office next to the sheriff's. Balls sat behind a wooden table. Two other uncomfortable chairs were in the room on the other side of the table. I took the one nearest the window. As soon as I sat down, Rick Schweikert came in, looking serious. His starched shirt actually glistened. After not-too-friendly greetings, Balls sighed and said, "Rick, I know you'd like to pin something on our writer here, but—"

"Now, Agent Twiddy, that's not necessarily so. What I want to do. . . ." He let his voice trail off when Balls held both hands up, palms outward.

"I know. What you want to do is wrap up the investigation into the death of Carter Lewiston. Now, you know and I know that Weaver here didn't have anything to do with that. And that's what's number one on the agenda. As for those, those remarks you've made concerning the death of the young woman, Tracy Keller, up in Washington area, well, that's just really bullshit."

Schweikert started to speak again but apparently thought better of it.

"Judging when she was shot and run off the road and when our Mr. Weaver here had fried okra at Southland, there just wasn't time for him to steal a car, run her off the road, get back to his own car and be down here."

I looked at Balls. Jesus, I thought. He checked out my story about eating at Southland.

Balls showed Schweikert the copy of a Visa printout from the restaurant. "Note the time, Rick."

Schweikert only glanced at the copy. But he wasn't going to be completely put off. "Just the same, Agent Twiddy, Mr.

Weaver here," he indicated me with a wave of his hand, "was seen accosting Carter Lewiston on the beach."

"Goddamnit, Schweikert, I told you I was trying to help the man. He'd just been beat up."

Balls made me shut up with one of his looks. Then to Schweikert he said, "And why beat up Lewiston, Rick? And then calmly go about fishing? And then do an execution-style killing of him a couple of days later? Aw, come on, Rick. Get real."

Schweikert slumped a bit in his chair, but without wrinkling his shirt in any manner. "I'll admit it doesn't. . . ." Then for the first time he showed something of his human side. "But damnit, Agent Twiddy, none of it makes sense. Why in God's name would anyone kill Carter Lewiston?"

Softly, Balls said, "That's what we've got to find out."

Schweikert stood. "Okay, this little gathering is over." He looked at me. "But I still don't like you. Remember that." He left the room.

Balls got that grin on his face. "I'd say the meeting went well, wouldn't you?"

"So you checked on me at Southland? I'm not sure that makes me feel so good."

Balls said, "Going up to Chesapeake anyway. Occurred to me they might remember you—the big tipper. Figured, too, that could shut Mr. Schweikert up. Even if the times don't really jibe that good." He chuckled. "When you don't have all the facts, bamboozle 'em with bullshit."

Then he sighed and put his hands palm down on the table. "But we're still not any closer to finding the guy who did in Lewiston—and your friend too, more than likely."

"More than likely, nothing. It's a sure thing."

He ignored me, appeared to be thinking. "I have found out a bit more about Mr. Lewiston's business ventures outside of the radio station."

I waited.

"First, we know that he and a few others have had an application in for some time to get clearance for the television station here. That's pretty much old news. But I also found out that he, along with a few other prominent types—including Gifford Grudgeon over near Hertford—have big plans for a government grant of some kind to build an ethanol plant in Northeast North Carolina. Somewhat hush-hush at this stage but one of the ladies there at the station sort of likes me."

"I've heard of Grudgeon. Lots of money, beer distributorship and other deals. Sort of a hardscrabble businessman, but aren't they all. The ones with money. So who're some of the others?"

Balls's eyes crinkled as he smiled. "Get this. The esteemed U.S. Congressman from over in the next district. The Honorable Jeremy J. Walston."

I shrugged. "This mean anything to you?"

The smile was gone. He shook his head. "Not a damn thing. Not yet, anyway."

Balls stood. I could see he had thickened a bit but still looked as tough as one of those heavyweight punching bags. "I got to get back over to Elizabeth City. This case is at the top of my list but unfortunately, it ain't the only one on that list."

"Okay," I said, "and I know you're dying to ask. Yep, I am going to stop downstairs and see Ms. Pedersen, ask her to dinner for tomorrow night."

Surprisingly, he got one of those rare, kindly expressions on his face, almost fatherly. "I'm happy for you, little friend."

Balls had shown great understanding and sympathy after Keely's death. I know he was pleased to see me moving on with life.

I did stop briefly downstairs. Elly came into the hallway to speak to me. We set a time for me to pick her up tomorrow night for dinner. "See you then, Harrison." There was a pause. "I guess I'd better get back in," she said.

I could see her two officemates peering out at us.

I smiled and nodded and went outside into the sunshine and stopped in at Manteo Booksellers to look around a bit before I headed back to Kill Devil Hills.

● ● ●

That afternoon a door to new possibilities for a fuller life opened for me, a life I had enjoyed in the past, but at the same time the door opened to the pain of remembrance.

I was at my computer when I saw an older model Buick pull into the cul-de-sac and nose partly into my driveway. I stood up so I could watch the man get out of the car. He appeared to be in his sixties. He wore khaki pants and a tan windbreaker over his sport shirt. His stomach bulged slightly over the belted khakis. I stepped out on the porch and he looked up at me, a smile on his face.

"Harrison Weaver?"

Trying not to sound too guarded, I said, "Yes?"

He walked a few steps closer. "I'm Jim Spencer. I play trumpet. I wanted to talk to you about music. Maybe playing. Ken Cavanaugh at *The Lost Colony* said you play bass."

I hesitated a moment, then said, "Come on up."

I met him at the top of my outside stairs. We shook hands standing just outside the door. His lower lip was full and the upper one almost delicately thin. Probably a good embouchure for a trumpet player.

He said, "I moved here from Richmond just a couple of months ago. Had a band up there off and on for years. Thought I'd given it up but got to thinking it'd be nice to get together a little combo—maybe two horns, piano and rhythm—woodshed a bit, and then play a few dinner-type gigs."

"Come on in the house."

He looked at my bass lying there on its side on the living room floor. "Nice instrument," he said.

I motioned for him to sit down on the sofa. I sat across from him in one of the chairs. "I haven't played jazz or with a combo in some time," I said. "As Cavanaugh knows, I played with mostly with a community symphony orchestra in Northern Virginia."

"Yeah, he mentioned that. But if you've played jazz or swing, and I'm talking about playing the standards mostly, you'd be able to get back into it real quick, I'm sure." He smiled and leaned forward. "I wish you'd think about it. I've got a sax man lined up, a drummer, and I think a piano player—or keyboard as he calls it."

"I've had my fill of playing in smoky nightclubs until all hours of the night," I said.

"Oh, me, too," he said quickly. "I'm talking about playing mostly for fun or taking dinner type jobs. Pick and choose." He began to get caught up in his enthusiasm. "And I believe we could pick and choose if we played the old standards. Lots of folks down here my age and older," he said with a grin. "They'd eat up music they remember."

The idea did have some appeal to me. It would open a new avenue, but still I held back a bit. "Let me think about it," I said.

He reached in the pocket of his windbreaker. "Here's a tape of my combo I had just before I moved down here. Listen to it. It's the stuff I'd like us to play."

We stood and he handed me the tape. "Think about it," he said. The smile was back. "I understand you're a freelance writer—so you won't have to quit your day job." He gave a short laugh.

We talked a bit further and he gave me one of his cards. I walked out to the stairway with him as he left, with a promise from me that I would at least think about it; as I said, the wood-shedding would be fun, getting together and polishing up some of the old standards.

When I went back inside I started to get back to the computer, but instead put the audio tape in my player. The recording was surprisingly good. I sat down to listen. The first piece was a medium swing version of "Sweet Lorraine." Jim Spencer did a nice mid-range chorus on it. Then the combo played an upbeat version of "Dancing Cheek to Cheek." That number brought back memories because I had played with a group that always did a jazz version of that tune, and once or twice Keely had sung with us. A touch of sadness nudged me.

But the next number did me in. The trumpet led off with a slow and melodic "Someone to Watch Over Me." Halfway through the first chorus I had to get up and turn the tape off. I could see and hear Keely singing that; it was one of her favorites, and mine too at the time. It was as if I were right there on the bandstand listening to her as she sang. The vision brought back such a flood of memories of her growing melan-cholia, her depression that led to her suicide, that I found my eyes tearing up. My chest actually hurt. I thought I would always be haunted by wondering if I really and truly watched over her as much as I could have.

I took the tape out of the player and stood there in the living room looking around as if I didn't know where to put it. I didn't want to destroy it, yet I couldn't listen to it again, not for a long, long time. I finally put it near the bottom of a stack of other tapes.

At that moment I didn't want to ever have anything to do with music again. But I knew even then, however, that the feeling would pass, eventually.

I would call Jim Spencer and tell him how busy I am now but that I would certainly keep it in mind.

On Saturday night I got over to Elly's about six. She had on a pale green polo shirt and trim tan slacks. As always, she smelled good, like sunshine and freshly laundered cotton. Martin started to tear up as we left but Mrs. Pedersen took his hand and distracted him.

We drove through Manteo and across the high bridge over Roanoke Sound. Without being obvious, I kept watch for suspicious vehicles. Except for that incident the other night in Manteo, I hadn't seen anything that aroused suspicion. Again, I reasoned, maybe it was just my imagination.

I told her about my visit from Jim Spencer and his wanting me to start playing again. I didn't tell her how depressed it made me to hear one of the songs. Elly said she would rather see me spending time playing with a bunch of guys in a band than getting all involved with murder investigations.

"Yeah, you could be a groupie," I said.

Several parking places were available at Sugar Creek Restaurant. Elly ordered flounder and I couldn't resist their lightly battered fried shrimp, sweetened tea.

Elly said, "When are you going up there? The memorial service."

"I'll have to leave Tuesday. Spend the night. Service will be at eleven Wednesday morning."

Elly nodded. "I'll be worried until you get back."

"I'll be vigilant," I said and smiled.

She gave a short mirthless laugh. "As a matter of fact, I'll be worried even *after* you get back—until the bad guy is caught."

"I don't think we need to worry. He's probably done all the bad stuff he intended." I knew it was a lie and that I didn't really believe that. Elly probably knew I was lying also but we let it go at that.

That night when I took her home and was kissing her goodnight in the living room, I held her tight against me and she moved in close to me. Then she gave me a smile and said softly, "Wow." With a chuckle she added, "I know . . . one of these days."

I was feeling great when I pulled out of her driveway and started toward 64. At the stop sign I waited for three cars that were headed toward Manteo. Then a car came up behind me, waiting for me to move on. In the mirror I could see that it was a sedan and that it was up close, so close I couldn't see the make. I didn't like the situation. The car behind me had seemed to come out of nowhere. As soon as the third car on 64 cleared, I pulled out quickly and turned right toward Manteo. I kept my eye on the mirror. The sedan behind me pulled out almost as quickly as I did, but it turned left toward the old bridge over Croatan Sound and Mann's Harbor.

It was a dark-colored late model Cadillac.

I spun my Saab around in a U-turn. But there were not even any taillights visible ahead of me. Disappeared. I drove another half a mile or so. Nothing. Then I made another turn-around and headed home.

But I kept watching.

I reached just under the front seat between my legs and pulled out the towel-wrapped revolver. I laid it on the seat beside me, its handle toward me. Every few minutes I put my hand on the revolver, like a strange security blanket—that might be needed.

Chapter Fourteen

Over the weekend I made reservations for Tuesday night at the Hilton in Fair Lakes. I was familiar with that area and could hop over to it off I-66.

Tuesday morning I left shortly after nine. I promised Elly I would call her from Northern Virginia. That night I ate at a Chinese Restaurant in Greenbriar Shopping Center where I was an old customer. The owner and the long-time waitress there greeted me like I was family. Back in the room, I called Elly, and also Balls to see if he had learned anything new.

"Nothing except that Lewiston had decided he wanted out of the ethanol project," he said.

After I hung up, something clicked in my mind. Hadn't Tracy told me that Mr. Mystery Man said something about Lewiston welching on a business deal? I started to call Balls back. Decided it was something I would talk to him about when I returned to the Outer Banks.

The next morning I was up and dressed early. For the first time in months I put on a tie. I checked the map again for the location of the church in Arlington. I arrived at the church a good twenty minutes or more before the service was scheduled to start. One of the first people I saw was big, heavyset Jean Clayborne. Her eyes were red. She gave me a hug, and then began to cry again. There must have been fifty or more in attendance. Very few of the other people did I know. Just as I took a seat on the aisle about midway down, I felt a tap on my shoulder.

It was Melvin Mellencamp, an absolutely pear-shaped young man about Tracy's age who had worked at Hand Gun Restriction. We all assumed he had always had an abiding un-requited crush on Tracy. She treated him with kindness because of his crush, but told me there was no way she could recip-rocate.

We shook hands. His eyes were red also, but I couldn't be sure whether it was from weeping or lack of sleep. "I want to talk to you afterwards," he whispered.

I nodded an okay. The urgency of his statement—it wasn't a request; it was a statement—stayed with me during the service. Several of Tracy's friends spoke. Invariably the word "irrepressible" came up during each of the eulogies. She was that—except at the end. The minister had never met Tracy. He did the best he could but he went on too long with what amounted to a sermon

Afterwards there was a reception downstairs in the fellowship hall of the church. I shook hands with a number of people I wasn't sure I really knew. Jean introduced me to several. I saw Melvin Mellencamp standing to one side. He had a cup of punch in one hand and a cupcake in the other. He stared at me. I excused myself from Jean and one of her friends and went over to Melvin.

He looked up at me, his expression intense. "You were with her just before it happened, Jean Clayborne said."

"Yes, I was."

He took a bite of the cupcake. Some of the icing smudged on his upper lip. "Mr. Weaver, do you think it was so-called road rage and a hit-and-run?"

I was puzzled. I thought by now it had certainly been revealed to all that she was shot before being slammed over the ravine. But maybe it wasn't common knowledge. I couldn't tell from his statement whether the road-rage referred to the shoot-ing as well. "What makes you ask that?"

"I know she was beat up. I called her. She told me a little about it. She wouldn't let me come see her. I think it was the same guy who beat her up, did her in, ran her off the road."

"Why are you telling me this? Maybe the police?"

"I wanted to get your opinion, Mr. Weaver."

"Stop the Mr. Weaver. Just Weav is fine."

"Okay. Everybody knows I really . . . I really liked Tracy." He pressed his lips tightly together in a show of trying to control his emotions. "Folks teased me about that. I didn't care. She was special, and I know she just sort of tolerated me. But she was nice to me." He chuckled. "She liked to hear me mimic the chairman and others." He did have a talent for that. He could mimic the voice and mannerisms of the Chairman of the House Agriculture Committee and other well-known congressmen flawlessly, including a former senator who had made a brief run for the presidency. You could close your eyes when he did it and swear you were listening to the actual person.

I said again, "But why are you asking me this? Why do you want my opinion?"

"I know you are an investigator or crime writer or something and I believe you may think the same thing. Maybe you know whether the police are any closer to solving it."

"I'm not an investigator. A former dirty-neck newspaper guy. And I live down in North Carolina now."

"I know where you live. And this thing may have North Carolina connections."

He had my attention.

One of the women from Hand Gun Restrictions came over to say she was glad to see me again, but not under these sad circumstances. We chatted a moment and then she moved on. I couldn't remember her name.

Melvin stood there patiently. He had finished the cupcake and wiped his fingers. He saw a tray and put down his empty cup and crumbled paper napkin, a blue one with white letters that said "The Lord is my Savior."

"Why do you mention a North Carolina connection?"

"To start with, you know I'm from North Carolina. Grew up in Williamston, and my mother lives right there in Manteo, works at the gift shop on Roanoke Island Festival Park." He paused. "And I'm not with Hand Gun Restrictions anymore. I'm back up on the Hill. I work for Congressman Jeremy J.

Walston of North Carolina. His chief of staff, matter of fact," he said with a touch of pride.

Bingo! The ethanol connection? This definitely had my attention.

Melvin looked around, lowered his voice. "That radio man that was killed, Carter Lewiston, the one Tracy said she was 'investigating,' was in a business venture with my boss, Congressman Walston."

"Yes?" As a reporter, I learned long ago that the fewer comments I would make, the more the other person would talk, fill in the gaps.

Melvin leaned close and whispered. I could smell blueberry cupcake on his breath. "I think my boss is worried about this whole thing."

I stared at him, waiting for him to say something else. He licked his lips, nervous.

"Mr. Weav, Tracy trusted you, so I know I can. Is there any way we can talk some more? Can you come up on the Hill? I've got to get back to the office. Boss has a hearing this afternoon. I've got to write his statement."

I told him I had planned to return to the Outer Banks. But I couldn't let this drop. No way. "Give me your office address," I said.

He gave me an address in the Longworth House Office Building.

"One or one-thirty?" I said.

"Fine. Hearing isn't until three."

In the meantime, I needed to call Balls—and Elly. If I got back tonight it was going to be late.

I ended up parking three long blocks away from Longworth and had a bit of a hike. Still I got to the Congressman's office a couple of minutes after one. At the receptionist's call, Melvin came out of an inner office to meet me.

"Have you eaten?" he asked. I started to answer but he quickly said, "Let's go down to the cafeteria and get a bite." He told the young woman at the reception desk that he would be back shortly. She gave a smile and then a look that said, "Sure you will."

I was going to take the stairs down but he suggested the elevator. He waddled when he walked. We both got hamburgers, and took a table off to ourselves. He had french fries and I helped myself to two of them that he hadn't doused with catsup.

"Okay, Melvin. What's this all about?"

"Now you've got to swear to God you'll keep this confidential."

"Hell, Melvin, I'm not swearing to anything until I know what it is. But discreet? Yes, I can promise that."

"That's good enough," he said. He took a bite of his hamburger, chewed thoughtfully, then said, "Start with, my boss hasn't done anything illegal. That's for sure. But I think he's into a situation that he wishes he wasn't."

"The ethanol project?"

Melvin nodded. "There's a big, I mean really big, government grant involved in getting the ethanol plant started. Plus some private donations as well. Corn farmers in Eastern North Carolina are really excited about it. Great market for as much corn as they can grow. Grant's being worked through the Tar Heel Economic Development Commission. Mr. Walston is big on alternative fuels, you probably know. So he saw this as a win-win situation. He lent his support to Gifford Grudgeon and a few other big names in Northeastern North Carolina who wanted this thing developed. The group included Carter Lewiston. My boss helped get the tracks greased for the grant."

I started to snitch another french fry, decided against it. They were disappearing fast. "So what's the problem? It does sound like a win-win situation."

He turned his big round face toward me and dabbed at a blob of catsup on his mouth.

I waited.

"I don't think there are any plans to build that ethanol plant. Never have been. And the Congressman doesn't think so either, at least he's beginning to."

"Take the money and run?"

"Basically, yes. More complicated than that. Hide it. Launder it. But, yes, take the money and run."

"And Carter Lewiston?"

"I think he found out that it was a scam and threatened to blow the whistle."

"So who killed Lewiston? And maybe Tracy, too?"

Melvin leaned forward. "I don't know. A hired hit man? I thought that was only in the movies."

I gave Melvin a hell of a hard look. "Just how much does the Congressman know?"

"Not much more than I do. In fact, I'm the one began nosing around and told the Congressman I was getting worried about the project, whether it was really legit or not. We've talked and now he's suspicious—and he's worried. Worried that the shit'll hit the fan. This thing gets out, you know."

"Christ, Melvin. You're not talking just political scandal. You're talking murder. Does your man understand that?"

"Yeah, of course he does," Melvin said, a touch of peevishness in his tone. "I mean he didn't have any part in this whole thing except to get the grant moving on a fast-track. Matter of fact, I'm the one did the real work on it. He lent his name."

I wasn't at all sure whether good ol' round 'n' rolly Melvin Mellencamp was telling me the truth about his boss. I said, "And just what do you expect me to do with this information, this suspicion of yours and the Right Honorable Jeremy J. Walston?"

"No sense in getting pissed off." He suddenly got rid of that baby-faced hurt look. His expression appeared to harden, an edge came into his voice. "It's pure and simple, Mr. Weaver. Tracy was special to you and to me. If what I've told you helps catch whoever did that to her, then it's . . . it's worth taking the risk of talking to you."

He looked me straight in the eye. I was still not convinced he was telling me all that he should. His reason for bringing me into his confidence had a murkiness to it that made me a bit uncomfortable. An editor at the beginning of my career used to drum into us to always ask yourself why a person was telling you what he was telling you. Just the same, I was beginning to have a bit more respect for Melvin Mellencamp, and I hoped it wasn't misplaced.

"Let's go talk to your boss," I said.

Melvin took a deep breath. "He's willing. He knows I'm talking to you, setting some of the groundwork, so to speak." He pulled out two napkins from the holder and wiped his hands.

Chapter Fifteen

Rep. Jeremy J. Walston appeared a very nervous little man when Melvin ushered me into his office, so I'm not sure how much of this "groundwork" Melvin had really laid down. I tried to put him somewhat at ease. I smiled and extended my hand. The Congressman's hand was damp but his grip was practiced and firm.

"To start with, Mr. Weaver, I want you to know that the only thing I had to do with this . . . this whole episode on the ethanol grant was just to help Gifford Grudgeon, one of my constituents, and his associates pave the way, so to speak, for a grant to build the plant. I'm very much interested in our great country developing alternative fuels so we're not dependent on those . . . on those folks in the Middle East."

"Yes, sir, I understand that."

He sat behind his massive desk that made him look even smaller. He moved a pen set to one side, then moved it back again.

He continued as if he'd practiced his speech. "Now Melvin here," and he nodded toward Melvin who sat slightly behind me in another chair to the side of his desk, "had heard rumors—and that's all they are, rumors—that there are no plans to actually build the plant. That distresses me. I believe Mr. Grudgeon is an honorable man. A good, honorable business-man." He toyed with the pen set again. "Now, I'll confess I don't know every single one of his associates in this venture. I do know that poor Carter Lewiston was one."

I nodded, waiting for him to continue.

Congressman Walston said, "I understand you're an investigator, and that—"

"Excuse me, Congressman. I'm a writer. I'm not an investigator. And I'm not a daily reporter any longer, so anything you tell me is just background."

"But your specialty is writing about things—being an investigative writer—that have certain unsavory elements to them."

"Yes sir, I write about murder and mayhem."

He pushed the pen set out of his reach. "After I learned of Mr. Lewiston's tragic death, and after talking with Melvin here, I called Mr. Grudgeon. He was as distraught as I was." Walston gave me one of his most sincere looks, one that would have made Bill Clinton proud. "I asked him point blank about rumors that there were no actual plans to build the ethanol plant. I can tell you, he was adamant about the fact that there was absolutely no truth to that. He said, 'I've got the plans right here on my desk.' He convinced me."

I couldn't keep quiet any longer. "Then, Congressman, with all due respect, just why are we having this conversation?"

He gave a little chuckle. "You could say that this is because my fine and loyal chief of staff, Melvin, believes that you may be able to help in some way find the person who did that violent thing to the young woman who was a friend of both of you—and in doing so, shed light on who committed that heinous crime against Carter Lewiston."

I thought a minute. "The police are working on both of these deaths."

For the first time, Melvin spoke up. "Pardon me, Congressman, for interrupting but let me say to Mr. Weaver that I believe he has a more personal interest in finding out what happened to Tracy, and to Mr. Lewiston, than the average overworked police officers."

Walston said, "That is a good answer to why we are having this conversation, which, incidentally—well, not so incidentally, either—Melvin has assured me you will keep in strictest confidence."

I nodded, but didn't say I agreed. Instead I said, "I need a list of the other persons involved with Gifford Grudgeon on this project."

"I'll call Gifford and tell him to make the list available to you," Walston said. Then he rose from his chair, still looking small behind the massive desk, signaling that the meeting was over.

We shook hands. The dampness was gone from his palm. His hand felt almost hot.

Melvin followed me outside into the hallway. "Do you feel okay about the meeting?" he asked.

"I don't know how I feel, Melvin, to tell you the truth." I stood there a moment, running something over in my mind. "I'm still not sure what was settled or uncovered or revealed in that meeting—other than the fact that the Congressman doesn't believe the rumor about taking the money and running. Or at least that's what he professes to believe."

Melvin said, "I hope he's as convinced as he sounds that it's all legit." Then he got one of those practiced looks of sincerity on his face. "But I am personally convinced that the Congressman is totally blameless if there are some shenanigans going on."

I wanted to get out of Washington as fast as I could. Good luck, I thought. Rush hour was never ending in Washington now. Even at three o'clock it appeared to be going strong as I headed south. God, I was glad I had moved to the Outer Banks. When I got near Fredericksburg, traffic on I-95 practically crawled. Once beyond the historic city that was now a bedroom community of Washington, my speed picked up again. I figured it would be close to nine before I crossed Wright Memorial Bridge back into Dare County and the Outer Banks.

When I could settle on driving without constantly keeping an eye on those around me, ahead of me, and behind me, I began to play over in my mind what if anything I had learned from meeting with Melvin Mellencamp and his Congressman boss.

Maybe it wasn't so inconsequential, after all. Maybe there was a glimmer there of what could have happened. If what Melvin suspected—and maybe the Congressman as well—that a scam of sorts was involved in the plans to build an ethanol plant, that could serve as a key to what happened to Carter Lewiston and then to Tracy. If someone didn't want word to get out on the scheme, and didn't want that word to get out bad enough, then possibly one of the participants in the project—and I had to get my hands on that list of players—might be the killer.

Or as Melvin said, maybe one of them hired someone who turned out to be a hit-man.

When I got on I-295, a loop around Richmond that connected to I-64 toward Newport News, I placed a call to Balls on my cell phone. Surprisingly he answered on the second ring. "Let's get together tomorrow," I said. "I've picked up some rumors in Washington that just might amount to something."

"Don't want to discuss it now?"

"Rather not on a cell phone, and besides I want to think it through a bit more and then see what your take is."

"Been having fun, huh?"

"Not exactly." The thought flashed through my mind of why I had gone to Washington to start with . . . Tracy Keller's memorial service.

Balls said he'd be driving to the Outer Banks from Elizabeth City first thing in the morning. We agreed he'd swing by the house, where we could talk privately.

Then I called Elly and told her everything was okay but it would be a bit late when I finally got to the Outer Banks. She said, "Call me anyway."

"It'll probably be after nine."

"Call me anyway, please."

I longed to be back at my little house. It was cozy, and Janey would chirp happily, and I might even play a few scales on the bass.

Death and murder and danger all seemed a long way away.

Chapter Sixteen

When I got in my house I locked up good. I put my .32 caliber revolver, which I'd started carrying in the car with me, atop the kitchen counter. I decided I ought to follow Balls' advice and get a *real* handgun.

Janey acted sullen. Didn't like being left alone. But after I spoke to her a while—and I was glad no one could hear me talking baby-talk to a parakeet—she came around and did her little head-bobbing dance.

I called Elly. She must have been right by the phone. "Got here and everything is fine."

"Lunch tomorrow?"

"I may be tied up with Agent Twiddy. I'll call tomorrow."

"Get a good night's sleep." She sounded sleepy.

As soon as I hung up the phone rang. I figured Elly had forgotten something and dialed me right back. I said a cheery hello.

But no one was there. Caller ID had been blocked.

Playing games?

I grilled a ham and cheese sandwich, which I almost burned watching *CNN Headline News*. At one point I muted the audio and listened for any activity outside. With the lamp by the sliding glass door off, I eased back a section of drape and peered into the night. All dark and quiet. I did play a few scales on the bass but it was a pretty desultory performance. I couldn't get with it.

Then, on something of a whim, I put the bow back in its leather holster on the tailpiece of the bass, and played a quick riff pizzicato, or plucking. It felt good. So I played a 12-measure blues in B-flat, then in C-major. I grinned because it made me feel better. I knew I had to get over the sadness associated with some of the tunes I used to play when Keely was with me. Taking a deep breath, I played a bass line from the first few chords of "Dancing Cheek to Cheek." There was a little sadness edging close to me, but not nearly as bad as I thought it might be. My fingers felt good and strong. In a way, as strange as it seems, it was as if playing pizzicato freed me from those hauntings of the past.

And Janey liked it too. She chirped and hopped around in her cage, hanging upside down a couple of times.

That night I slept well. Good to be back in my own bed. I realized that was a sign I was getting rather set in my ways. The next morning I was up and showered and dressed in khakis and golf shirt, boat shoes with no socks, waiting for Balls.

With the drapes open, I had a view of the cul-de-sac and could see any vehicle that approached. A new Ford pickup truck pulled into my street and stopped just inside my driveway. I stepped out on the deck just as a lanky young man got out of the pickup. He had on jeans, a T-shirt and wore his hair in a short ponytail.

"Mr. Weaver? Morning."

I nodded a rather cautious greeting.

He peered up at me, cupping one hand to shade his eyes. "Came to inquire about your boat. I understand you're about to put it on the market at a good price."

I walked down the steps. On a trailer beside the house I have a practically new 18-foot Ranger Reata, which I haven't had in the water in more than a month. I have a beat-up old Jeep with a hitch for towing it short distances. Don't try to use the Saab for that task. There's a public launch area less than half a mile from the house.

He put out his hand.

"Where'd you hear I might be considering selling my boat?"

"Fellow down at the Front Porch Café. Heard me talking to one of the gals there. He came up. Real friendly guy. Said he knew where a boat was that was going on the market at a really good price. Practically a new boat."

I slowly shook my head.

"Sounded like he was a friend of yours. Knew your name, where you live, and everything."

"What was his name?"

"You know, I never asked him. Big guy. Southern, but not from around here didn't sound like. Dressed nice."

"I don't have any plans to sell the boat," I said.

The young man shrugged, looked a little puzzled, as if he was not sure he believed me. "That's funny. Seemed he knew all about it. We stood outside the café talking a bit, weather and stuff. Then he drove off." The young man put his hand out again. "Well, if you change your mind, I'd like to talk to you about your boat there."

"What was he driving?"

"Huh?"

"This guy you were talking to. What was he driving?"

"Practically a new Cadillac. Dark blue one, I think. Needed washing, but a nice car."

He left and I went back inside and locked the door. I felt a trickle of perspiration slide down my side. Maybe just for comfort, I put my hand on my pea-shooter revolver, hefted its weight.

Playing with me. Playing games. I knew he wouldn't stop. This was fun to him.

Less than a half hour later Balls drove up in his Thunderbird, turned around in the cul-de-sac and backed into the driveway, nose out.

I stepped out on the deck. Balls wore a jacket and tie. Real business today, it appeared. When he came up the steps I pointed at my boat. "A guy just came and wanted to buy it."

"Give you a good offer?"

"It's not for sale. But this fellow knew my name, had my address. Said he met someone at the coffee shop, a real friendly guy, who told him I was putting my boat up for sale this week-end at a good price."

"Yeah?" Balls said, lifting one eyebrow.

"This real friendly guy who told him Mr. Weaver had a boat for sale was driving a late-model Cadillac, dark colored. The fellow didn't get his name but got the feeling apparently he wasn't local."

Balls looked hard at me. "Let's step inside," he said.

Balls stepped over the neck of my bass and sat on the couch. I sat in the chair by the phone, facing him.

"He's got me targeted, Balls. This is his idea of foreplay." I know I sounded a bit unnerved, and I was.

Balls was quiet a moment. He nodded toward the kitchen counter. "I see you've got your peashooter handy."

"Yeah. If it still works."

Balls sighed, leaned back in the sofa and looked at me. "I think you better stick sort of close to me for a while." Then, "And we're going to find this son of bitch."

Exactly how we were going to do that, I had no idea, and I'm sure Balls didn't either.

He got up and came to the phone. I scooted my chair over a bit. I saw that he punched in the sheriff's office and apparent-ly got Mabel. "This is Agent Twiddy. Put the word out that if any of the deputies see a dark blue or black late model Cadillac, driven by a lone Caucasian male, in his forties, pull it over, get the registration info, name and license number." He listened a moment. "No, just tell them we're checking for someone. If they do, you radio or call me back on my cell." He gave the number. "Thanks, Mabel."

He went back to the sofa. "Okay," he said, "tell me about yesterday."

I told him about Melvin Mellencamp approaching me at the memorial service, saying he wanted to talk, the meeting with him at the Longworth House Office Building, and then the visit with Rep. Jeremy J. Walston.

Balls shook his head. "Why did Melvin, and especially the Congressman, want to tell you all of this?"

"Melvin said he figured that I wanted to put the finger on whoever killed Tracy, and thought I could help. Referred to me as an investigator. Told him I wasn't, that I was a writer."

I paused a moment, playing over Melvin's whole demeanor in approaching me and talking to me. "You know, now that I think about it, it seems that Melvin was more interested in talking about the ethanol plant and whether we were closer to figuring out who did this than he was in. . . ." I let my voice trail off. "I don't know, he just didn't seem as broken up about Tracy as I thought he would've been. I mean this was her memorial service, for God's sake."

Balls dismissed this with a shrug. "Go on."

"Melvin said he had heard rumors that getting the grant for the ethanol plant was just a scam. That it wasn't going to be built. Then Walston tried to disavow this in a way. Said he had checked with Gifford Grudgeon, and Gifford said he had plans right on his desk. Walston promised to tell Grudgeon to make the list of participants in the ethanol project available to me."

Balls sat there thinking it over. "Still seems strange to me that Walston would even talk to you about it."

I said, "His trusted staffer, Melvin, set him up for it, I'm sure."

Balls pursed his lips. "Or maybe the Congressman was just trying to show you how open and cooperative he was."

Neither of us said anything for a minute or so. Then Balls stood, hitched up his slacks, "Tell you what let's do. . . ."

"Go see Gifford Grudgeon," I said.

"You got it. Better call the old bastard first. And I've got to stop by the sheriff's office briefly see what Albright or any of his deputies might have found out on the Lewiston investigation." He shook his head again, a mannerism that appeared to be more frequent lately. "Then I got to focus on the late Mr. Lewiston. About to wind up with the Elizabeth City thing."

Balls placed a call to Grudgeon's primary business, Columbia Beverage Company, over on the mainland beyond East Lake. He spoke to Grudgeon's secretary and identified himself. He didn't ask for an appointment; he simply told her that he and Harrison Weaver were coming over to see Mr. Grudgeon on a matter that Congressman Walston had called him about. Then he signed off before she had an opportunity to register any comment or objection. To me, he said, "Gifford will be there. Curiosity if nothing else."

I said, "I'd better at least put some socks on if we're going to see one of the area's leading businessmen."

When I came back in the living room and we prepared to go, Balls stood peering down at Janey's cage. "You hear that?" he asked. "That bird said 'shit' just as plain as anything."

"Naw, female parakeets don't talk."

"Well, that little bitch did."

Janey could tell she was getting attention. She made a non-musical chirping sound, followed by, "Bitch."

"Don't tell me you didn't hear that. She's mocking me."

"Didn't hear a thing, Balls."

The console in Balls' car was cluttered with radio equipment. I sank back in the seat as he gunned the Thunderbird out ahead of traffic on the Bypass. He grinned.

Balls said, "Changed my mind." Using the speaker phone, he called the sheriff's office. "Mabel, tell the sheriff I'm headed over to the mainland and would like to stop by to see him when I get back, oh, about two o'clock. Okay?"

When he disconnected, I said, "Thought you were going to stop by there on the way."

"Well, that was just so you could see the Pedersen gal. But if you can wait until we take care of this other business, we'll swing by there then. Think you can wait?"

"Screw you, Balls."

He chuckled, having fun.

We drove south on the Bypass to Whalebone Junction, swung right toward Roanoke Island, across the Baum Bridge and reached the relatively new bridge that serves as a more effective evacuation route in case of a hurricane than the only other one that required going through the town of Manteo.

We hadn't talked for a while when Balls said, "Tell me why you think your friend Tracy was killed by our mystery man, if in fact he is the one who did it."

I had thought a lot about it. "He enjoyed it. He's an evil son of a bitch and he enjoyed killing her. He enjoyed beating her up. He didn't have to kill her. She didn't even know his name."

Balls glanced at my face and then concentrated on the road again.

I said, "Now assume he's the same one who killed Carter Lewiston, and I don't think there's any question about that, then I can see maybe he kills Lewiston to keep him quiet. But why beat him up first, then come back to kill him a couple of days later? Make Lewiston worry about it? More of this business of playing with his victim?"

Balls moved the Thunderbird easily around a vacationer's minivan, keeping the speed up close to seventy.

Then I said, "And another thing about this bastard that occurs to me—and it may seem like a stretch—but I think he likes to send a message. When he killed Tracy after she met with me, was he sending me a message? This sighting of what I think is his Cadillac and the business about my boat this morning, are those his ways of sending me a message?"

"Make you a bit edgy?" Balls asked.

"Damn right."

As we pulled into the graveled parking lot at Columbia Beverage, workers loaded cases of beer onto one of Grudgeon's beer trucks. A Toyota Camry and a Jeep Cherokee nosed in toward the front entrance. Balls swung around and backed in expertly beside the Camry.

As if to set the stage as to why I was along, Balls said, "I brought you because you are the one who visited the Congressman and the reason he called Grudgeon about the list of people involved."

I nodded.

A middle-age woman, looking as if she suffered no nonsense from anyone, eyed us and mumbled something of a greeting.

With a smile, Balls told her who we were—I'm sure she already suspected—and that we were there to see Mr. Grudgeon.

"Just a minute," she said, without returning the smile, and eased herself out from behind her rather grimy looking desk and stepped into the office behind her, reclosing the door as she did. A moment later she came back and said we could go in now.

Gifford Grudgeon stood up as we entered. A big man, as tall as Balls, thick in the middle, with a large coarse-skinned face that appeared could never be shaved properly. Salt and pepper hair that wouldn't be tamed properly, either.

But he smiled broadly and warmly, almost as if he was amused by our visit. He motioned us to wooden chairs near the front of his desk. His desk didn't look much better than his secretary's.

He asked us if we'd like coffee, a soda, or a beer.

"No, we're fine," Balls said.

Actually, I wouldn't have minded having a Coke or Pepsi. But I didn't say anything. Smiling and looking pleasant was the order of the day.

Grudgeon said, "Now, I don't believe in wasting a whole lot of time on chit-chat, unless we're out on a boat fishing or drinking some beer, so tell me exactly why I've got the pleasure of your presence here this glorious day." He looked at me. "Both of you." His manner of speaking flowed more smoothly than the lines on his face.

Before Balls could speak, Grudgeon spoke up again. "I believe it has to do with that thing that Jeremy—Congressman Jeremy Walston—called me about. A list of participants in the great ethanol project."

Balls leaned forward and spoke up quickly, taking advantage of the slight pause. "Yes, sir, that's part of it."

Grudgeon eyed him. "What's the other part?"

"Oh, we'd like to chit-chat a bit about the great ethanol project, who's involved, that sort of thing. And I thought maybe we could all express our sympathy about the unfortunate demise of one Mr. Carter Lewiston." Balls wasn't to be outdone.

Grudgeon apparently enjoyed the game. He smiled appreciatively at Balls. But then he said, "What's so curious to me, though, is why Jeremy sent you to me for the list. He knows who they are. Hell, his wife is one of them and so is his wife's brother. He knows good as me who's involved."

From Balls, a noncommittal, "I see."

"As you probably know, I've got this little business here and a number of other projects as well, including a right sizable amount of farmland, both owned and leased, that could profit handsomely from a corn-fed ethanol plant. Hell, those big boys like ADM and Cargill don't need to be the only ones benefiting from Uncle Sam wanting to get into the alternative fuel business."

I said, "Excuse me Mr. Grudgeon, but Congressman Walston indicated to me that his role was solely that of sort of greasing the tracks, so to speak, to speed up the federal grant for this project."

"Well, on paper that's probably true. But his wife's involved, and his brother-in-law."

Balls moved his right hand down by his side and flicked his fingers toward me, which I correctly took as a sign he wanted me to keep my mouth shut. "What about Carter Lewiston? He was one of the participants?" Balls asked.

"Sure was. Jeremy had this idea that if we had some prominent, well-known people involved, it might go faster. Carry more weight. Now as far as what happened to Carter, I haven't a clue." He chuckled, "And I don't believe you do either. No insult intended."

Grudgeon produced a sheet of paper from under a paperweight shaped like a cartoon pig with the name of an area barbecue pit on its base. "Here's that list of folks involved, with Carter's name drawn through. Names and addresses. Not but seven of us. Six now." He laid the list on the edge of the desk.

Balls took the list and studied it quietly.

Grudgeon nodded at me, "Heck, Jeremy could have given you this list when you were up in Washington with him. Save you all the trouble of coming over here."

Balls said, "Wanted to talk to you anyway, Mr. Grudgeon. For one thing, there are rumors that once the grant is finalized, there are no real plans to actually build an ethanol plant."

Grudgeon shook his head and chuckled to himself. "I think I know exactly where those rumors started coming from. They came from that little fat boy Jeremy has on his staff, that Melvin . . . Mellon-something . . . maybe Melvin Watermelon. That's what he looks like."

Then Grudgeon leaned forward, put his arms on his desk, stared straight at Balls. "Now think about this, Agent Twiddy. If that plant gets built and up and running and this whole area begins to prosper more, and God knows it can use it, and I start selling more beer and sodas, and my two little grocery stores start making more money, and my houses get rented to good, hard-working folks, and on top of all that if I can sell as much corn to that plant as I can grow on land that I own or that I lease, I'd stand to make a whole hell of lot more money than if I scooted off with one-seventh or one-sixth of a federal grant, and I don't give a damn how big the grant is. I'm in business to make money so as I can enjoy life, and I'm in business to make money for a long, long time. I ain't planning to grab a handful of dollars and scamper off to Mexico or some other god-forsaken place."

Balls said, "Good statement, Mr. Grudgeon. I can follow your reasoning. Just two more questions and we'll let you get back to your business . . . of doing business.

"First, as you say, since I probably don't have a clue about Mr. Lewiston's death, tell me if *you* have any idea why a man like Mr. Lewiston would be killed in what appeared to be an execution-type slaying. Was he into anything that you know of that would have caused this to happen?"

Grudgeon said, "I'm serious, Agent Twiddy. It has puzzled the hell out of me, too. I've never heard a blasted bad thing about him. Straight arrow. Little sissy acting, but, you know, classical music and all of that. Don't mean anything by that. He was married once, I know, has a couple of kids, high school or college."

Balls said, "Do you think maybe he was about to blow the whistle on this ethanol project."

Grudgeon's face reddened in anger. "Now you're beginning to piss me off, Twiddy. There's no goddamn whistle to blow."

"Okay, okay. Withdrawn."

"You said there were two questions. What's the other one and then I got to get back to running a business."

"Who's in charge of this ethanol project? Who's the top man of the group? You?"

Grudgeon's color had come back to its more normal country-boy ruddiness. "Not me. They talked about me spearheading it, so to speak. Take someone with more time than I've got. As a matter of fact, I suggested we have a chairman and vice chairman, maybe a secretary-treasurer, too."

Balls had glanced again at the list he held in his big paw of a hand. "Who then?"

"That's sort of interesting now that you bring it up," Grudgeon said. "One with the most time on his hands is Jeremy's brother-in-law Steve Partens. Jeremy's wife, Hilda, sort of an unofficial vice chair, and our departed Carter Lewiston was the secretary-treasurer."

Balls stood and I took it as a clue to do the same. "Thank you, Mr. Grudgeon for your time on such short notice. This has been helpful."

Grudgeon put out his hand. "Pick up a beer or a soda from the cooler out front on your way out," he said.

But Balls didn't stop, even though I eyed the cooler sitting on a small table beside Miss Grumpy's desk.

Chapter Seventeen

We drove a minute or so without speaking. Balls reached inside his jacket pocket for the list of participants, handed it to me.

I unfolded the single sheet and read the names and addresses listed. Only three of the individuals we didn't already know about. I recognized the names. A big real estate developer and former county commissioner from the Outer Banks; the owner of a topnotch boat-building operation toward Edenton; and the owner of a large auto dealership just north of the Outer Banks and another dealership in Elizabeth City.

And then there was Hilda Walston, wife of the Congressman, and her brother, Steve Partens. I broke the silence. "These other three don't sound like they'd need to risk trying to pull off a scam, any more than Grudgeon does."

Balls puffed out a breath of air. "If there's such a thing as a plan for a goddamn scam." Frustration put an edge to his voice. "Let's get your fat boy friend on the phone, ask him about this rumor of his, and also when's the Congressman coming back to the area. Would like to pay him a visit at home . . . see his wife *and* that brother-in-law. You got Walston's number?"

"Just dial the main switchboard at the Capitol, 202-224-3121, ask for his office."

"You dial," he said. "Putting you on speaker."

When I got through to Walston's office, there was a pause of several seconds and then Melvin Mellencamp came on. "Melvin, this is Harrison Weaver. I'm in the car with SBI

Agent Ballsford Twiddy. We've just been to see Gifford Grudgeon, and now there are two things we'd like to ask you."

Guardedly, "Yes?"

"First, when is the Congressman coming back to the home area so we can visit with him?"

"Oh, that's easy. He'll be there Friday afternoon and all weekend. Matter of fact I'm coming with him. I got to work on a speech for him."

"That's good. We'll arrange to see him and you. We'd also like to chat with Mrs. Walston and her brother."

He paused, then said, "I'm sure that can be arranged. And the second question?"

"We want to know where you heard that rumor, you know, about the ethanol plant and plans concerning it?"

"Oh, I'd rather not say. . . ."

Balls couldn't keep quiet any longer. "Listen, Melvin, this is SBI Agent Twiddy. Frankly, I don't care whether you'd rather say or not. I want to know. Now you can tell me now or I'll be all over you this weekend. You understand me?"

A rather weak, "Yes sir." Then I could tell that he had perhaps cupped his hand over the mouthpiece so others nearby couldn't hear him. "It was my mother. The rumor came from my mother."

Balls again, "You *mother*?"

"Yes sir. She happens to be a long-time good friend of Carter Lewiston's. *Was* a long-time friend. Real good friend. He must have said something to her. She passed it on to me. She said Carter was real upset."

I spoke up, "Melvin, I wish you'd told me that when I was up there."

"Well, you didn't ask me, for one thing, but I don't know I'd of told you then, anyway."

Didn't ask him? No, I don't believe I did. Hell of a reporter I am.

"Melvin, this is Agent Twiddy again. Why didn't the Congressman just go ahead and give Weaver a list of participants instead of sending him down to see Gifford Grudgeon?"

Again the hand cupped over the mouthpiece, "Tell you the truth, Agent Twiddy, I wondered that myself at the time."

Balls drew a finger across his throat, signaling to end the conversation. I said, "Okay, Melvin. Appreciate it. Listen, I'll be back with you later today, after you've had a chance to speak to the Congressman, to set a time to visit with him down here."

Balls clicked the phone off. I waited for him to get his thoughts together and speak. We drove for a couple of miles before he said, "I'll tell you, Weav, either the Congressman is just trying to distance himself, or his wife, or he's playing games with us. We'll find out." He rubbed his moustache with the fingers of one hand. "Maybe there is something to this scam business. And maybe if the Congressman isn't in on it, maybe he suspects his wife is—or her loving brother."

"What now?"

Balls glanced at his watch. "Shit, let's get something to eat."

He placed a call to the sheriff's office. "Mabel, anybody spot that Cadillac? Well, keep it out there, not as a priority. Just sort of curious." When he signed off, he said to me, "He's probably long gone, crawled back in his hole where he hides."

When we got back to Manteo we continued past Budleigh Street to Darrell's Restaurant and got in with the last of the lunch crowd. Neither one of us could pass up their special on lightly breaded popcorn shrimp.

After we had eaten and headed back to the courthouse, Balls said, "I'm going up to see the sheriff, fill him in on what damn little I know. See if any of his deputies have come up with anything on Lewiston, which I doubt." He pulled into the reserved spot and grinned like Tom Selleck. "So why don't you go see your gal Elly in the meantime. I know you're just squirming to go see her."

I gave him a look.

"Just don't drool all over her," he said as I got out of the car.

When I stepped into Elly's office, one of the other women called musically, and with a touch of tease in her voice, "Elly, someone to see you."

Elly came out from the little inner office, gave me a big smile.

"You got time for a cup of coffee?" I asked.

"Sure." To the others she said, "I'll be back in just a few minutes."

"Take your time, Elly," the musical-voiced one said. "I certainly would," and she gave a little laugh, as did the other woman.

Outside, Elly said, "They think you're cute."

"Cute? My God, that's for youngsters. What about this touch of gray, and the wrinkled brow?"

"Gives you character," she said, and we made our way across the street from in front of Manteo Booksellers to the coffee shop upstairs. We sat on the rather faded but comfortable sofa with our espressos.

I didn't give her any details other than that I had been out with Balls. I started to tell her about the incident with the boat this morning, but thought better of it.

Instead I looked at the way the afternoon sun came in through the window and touched her cheek and the back of her neck. I always marveled at how fresh she looked.

"What are you looking at? My hair messy?"

"Just admiring you."

She smiled. "Well, stop it. It makes me nervous."

"I like making you nervous. Getting you upset."

She stirred her coffee with the tiny spoon. "I know," she said. "I know."

Before we left, she got very serious. "Harrison, I want you to be careful. Real careful. That man's still out there. You're the only one around here who has seen him—at least that we know of. You know and I know that puts you in danger."

Once again I said what I didn't really believe, "Maybe he's done what he came to do and has left."

When we went back to Elly's office, the musical-voiced woman said, "Agent Twiddy said that when you two come back—if you come back—he's ready to go."

"I'll call upstairs to Mabel," Elly said.

"Be waiting for him at his car," I said and told her I would call later.

With her hand at her waist so the other women couldn't see, she wiggled her fingers goodbye.

All Balls said when he got in the car was, "Nothing. Not a damn thing."

On the way back to Kill Devil Hills to drop me off, Balls said, "Let's call Melvin again, get that appointment for Saturday morning."

Melvin already had it set up. We would see the Congressman at his home near Hertford at ten o'clock Saturday morning. Melvin gave me directions over the speaker phone. Balls mouthed that he already knew where it was.

I could tell Balls was exasperated with the way things were going, or not going. "I gotta get back over to Elizabeth City," he said.

He turned the car around in the cul-de-sac at my house. He stared for a moment at me. "Stay out of trouble. Anything suspicious, call me on my cell."

I nodded and started unfolding myself out of the Thunderbird.

He reached over, put his hand on my arm and said quietly, "And keep that little peashooter handy. I mean it. Real handy."

Chapter Eighteen

When I got inside and checked on Janey, got a glass of iced tea, I suddenly felt tired. I kicked my boat shoes off and stretched out on the sofa. But I took the revolver and laid it on the coffee table beside me. I went sound asleep.

When I woke up, dusk was coming on. I closed the drapes and turned on the outside lights. I gave Janey fresh water and a sprig of millet seed. She chirped and said, "Shit."

I said, "Female parakeets don't talk. Don't you know that?" She chirped and did her head-bobbing.

Another tomato sandwich. Well, it was something and I had a good lunch. I flipped on the television and surfed through the channels. Settled on the news, turned the volume down after a couple of minutes, and then went to my computer. Didn't feel like working but I had to force myself into it. Once I got started, though, it went well. The time slipped by. The news was long off, so was *Jeopardy*, and a rerun of *Law and Order* was well into nailing a suspect when the phone rang and made me jump.

The caller ID was blocked. I figured it was a telemarketer. But when I answered, the polished, syrupy Southern accent on the other end of the line made a chill run down my back.

"Real shame what happened to your lady friend up there in Washington. That's a dangerous place."

"Who is this?" My voice sounded uneven.

"Oh, buddy boy, you know who it is." Then, "You going fishing anytime soon? Might be better fishing today than it was last week when you were out there."

"Listen, you son of a bitch. . . ."

"Now, no sense in talking that way. Here I am trying to give you advice about fishing and you're calling me vile names."

My jaw muscles were so tight they hurt. "You're a cowardly bastard, beating up older guys and young women. Why don't you show yourself? Don't have the guts?"

He chuckled. "Oh, I've shown myself. You know that. You've seen me around. Just that I'm always busy and can't stop and chat with you."

"You can't stay hidden."

"Buddy boy, I don't intend to stay hidden." He said it with a new coldness. "Now reason I'm giving you advice about the fishing is that tomorrow, now, ocean's going to be a different thing altogether. Understand a blow's coming through tonight, cause overwash on the Beach Road, deadly rip currents, too. You don't want to get out in that. Ocean can be a killer."

Then his voice lost the trace of good-ol'-boy Southern accent. "And don't even try to have this call traced to find out where it came from. Won't do you any good at all." He chuckled again, the accent back: "And I'm not far from you. Not far at all. So's I can keep an eye on you."

The phone clicked off. I put the receiver down slowly. A dampness from my palm was visible on the handset.

I picked the phone up again and dialed Balls' cell phone. He clicked on after two rings. "Yeah?"

"He called me, Balls. He's playing with me." I gave Balls a complete rundown of what was said.

"I'm calling the sheriff's office. Get an unmarked to come to your place, park all night in the cul-de-sac."

"I don't think he's through playing games."

"Maybe not. Maybe so. My advice stay right there in the house. I'll be down in the morning." He got a lighter tone to his voice that was supposed to make me feel better. "And sure as shit don't go fishing in the ocean."

I made sure all of the blinds and the drapes were closed, all lights on outside, sliding glass door and the kitchen door locked. I slipped the little revolver in my pants pocket. It felt heavy but it gave a degree of comfort. I did a lot of pacing around the house. Turned the television off. Sat on the sofa for a while and then got up to see if the unmarked car had arrived.

Less than thirty minutes later the phone rang. I looked at caller ID, local number.

"Mr. Weaver, this is Deputy Odell Wright. I'm about three minutes from your place. I'll blink my lights so you'll know it's me." A smile sounded in his voice. "That way you won't shoot at me."

"Sorry you're having to do this, Odell."

"Don't worry about that. I'll keep a sharp eye."

"I know you will, and thanks, my friend."

Through the side of one of the blinds in the dining area near my computer, I kept watch and saw Deputy Wright pull into the cul-de-sac, blink his lights twice and then back his car to where it was partially hidden by a live oak tree on the west side of my house.

By ten o'clock the wind had started blowing hard from the northeast. Yes, a northeaster was blowing in. If I concentrated on listening, I could hear the surf kicking up. There would be overwash on the Beach Road, piles of blown sand and ocean foam. With the wind like this if you tried driving down the Beach Road your car would become speckled with salty foam.

I tried to work but couldn't get with it, so gave up for the night. I took another shower, standing in the hot water for several minutes. When I finally went to bed I didn't think I would be able to sleep, but I did. Waked at three-twenty and looked outside again at Odell Wright's car, went back to bed. It was fully light when I got up and fixed coffee and took a cup down to Odell.

As often happens, the nor'easter had blown through and now the wind had shifted to the northwest and the skies began to clear.

Odell looked tired but fully awake, with the driver's window rolled down. The morning light glistened a bit on his whiskers. I was surprised to see some gray mingled in and looking silvery against his dark skin.

"Time for you to go off duty, isn't it, Odell?"

"I talked to the dispatcher. I'm going to hang around until Agent Twiddy gets here. He's already on his way. Probably burning the road with that souped-up T-Bird of his."

"Want something to eat?" I asked.

"Thanks, no, Mr. Weaver. I'll stop down the road when I leave here."

"What's this 'Mister' business? It's Weav or Harrison to my friends."

He grinned. "Gotcha."

"Hell, as one of the original Wright Brothers you don't need to be formal, you know."

He chuckled. "I am going to get out and stretch a bit."

I nodded toward the house. "Bathroom?"

"Naw. What you think God made live oaks for?"

I went back in the house and finished getting ready for the day. Within twenty minutes, Balls' Thunderbird swung into the cul-de-sac, wheeled around and backed into my driveway. He did make good time, or left awfully early.

He spoke to Odell for a few minutes. I stood on the deck. Odell looked up and waved, got in his cruiser and drove away. Balls came up the steps that run along the side of the house, no smile on his big face.

He plopped down on the sofa.

"Coffee?"

He shook his head. "I got a feeling we're getting close to show time."

I took my coffee and sat across from him, waiting.

"He's not there yet," Balls said, "but he's got something planned." He studied the way Janey nibbled at her cuttlebone. Then, "And it may not be you he's aiming at. I think he likes letting you know he's in charge, or thinks he is."

"Seems like right now he *is* pretty much in charge."

"I think I will have a cup of coffee," he said.

I started to get up.

"Naw, I'll get it." He moved toward the kitchen. "Don't you ever pick that goddamn bass fiddle up off the floor?"

When he came back to the sofa, he said, "You hang around with me today. I think it's best. We're going to the sheriff's and tell him about your call last night. I think he's beginning to be a believer—that this mystery man ain't something you dreamed up."

When we got to the Budleigh Street side of the courthouse, Balls slid the Thunderbird into the last remaining reserved spot. We went in the side, non-public, entrance, and up the back stairs. Mabel shuffled out of the sheriff's office, limping a bit on her swollen ankles. She wore those soft black shoes she favored, and a big smile of greeting for us.

Then she nodded over her shoulder toward the sheriff's closed door. "Mr. Schweikert's in there. But they're expecting you."

Balls looked at me, shrugged, tapped on the door and opened it.

Schweikert sat on one of the wooden chairs near the window. For the first time, his shirt didn't look quite as stiffly starched as usual. In fact, *he* didn't look as stiffly starched. He bobbed his head slightly in greeting, hardly looking at me.

Sheriff Albright half-raised his bearlike frame from behind his desk and extended his hand.

Balls and I took the two remaining chairs, with Balls close to the sheriff's desk.

Albright settled back in his leather chair and sighed. "Mr. Schweikert was just telling me about an interesting phone call he had last night."

Balls turned to Schweikert. "You got a call?"

Schweikert nodded solemnly. "About eight forty-five. ID was blocked. But a man—Southern accent, probably Caucasian—spoke very politely and said, and this is just about a direct quote, 'Mr. Schweikert, I certainly don't mean any disrespect, but aren't you distressed that Mr. Carter Lewiston's killer is still out there? I know I would be if I were in your shoes.' I said who is this? and he didn't even bother to answer. Then he said, 'I quite fervently hope that this person doesn't, you know, do away with any other of your dear—or not so dear—citizens.' Then he hung up."

Schweikert, who usually had a strict military bearing, actually appeared to sag, as if his shoulders had suddenly become weary.

Balls was the first to speak, "Just before he placed that call to you, he apparently called Weaver. Has to be the same guy. He's our killer. You got a call from the killer, and so did Weav."

Balls asked me to relate what had been said to me on the phone last night.

Schweikert watched me as I talked. When I finished, he said, "Weaver, I don't like you a bit more today than I ever have, but . . . well, at any rate, I'm not looking at you as a suspect." He tried to force a wry smile. "At least not yet."

Balls said, "This guy's just playing with us. He's having fun."

Albright said, "He's the only one having fun."

"Thing about it is, he's not through," Balls said. "He's got someone else in his sights. And he wants us to know that."

Chapter Nineteen

Before we left the sheriff's office, Balls requested another deputy be posted outside my place tonight.

Schweikert said, "What about me? Think I may need some protection?"

Balls said, "My opinion is, no. He doesn't have any reason to target you. He just wanted to bug you, get you stirred up. Weav here knows what he looks like. He's been following Weav. He has a reason to want him . . . ah, not to remember him anymore."

"Thanks, Balls. That really makes me feel good," I said.

Before we left his office, the sheriff indicated he would like to speak to Balls privately for just a moment. Schweikert, his military bearing once again more or less firmly in place, strode past me, headed to his office. I waited in the hall. I really wanted to step downstairs and at least say hello to Elly but I figured I'd better wait for Balls.

Mabel came hobbling by and stopped.

"How you been, Mabel?"

"Oh, fair to middlin', I guess. No sense in complaining, is it?" She gave a deep but not loud chortle. "But since you asked. . . ."

"No, really," I said. "I'm asking."

"Feet and legs. Carrying all this weight around for years. I've given up on dieting. Enjoy my food too much." She nodded toward the sheriff's closed door. "Making any progress on poor Mr. Lewiston?"

I shook my head.

Balls came out of the sheriff's office. I told Mabel good-bye. Balls patted her shoulder. We started down the backstairs. I didn't mention wanting to see Elly. I was surprised Balls didn't bring it up, but he seemed preoccupied.

We got outside and Balls said, "Ride with me down to Wanchese. Get down there you can stay in the car or look at some of those big boats you'll probably buy when you sell your next book."

"Yeah," I said. "In my dreams."

As we headed south on the Wanchese road, it was like stepping back in time. Most of the houses were far from modern, and many less than modest, with rusting crab pots and a number of older boats in dire need of repair and paint. But with the relatively new Seafood Park, expert boat-building facilities, the area had come a long way in a few years. It was the commercial fishing center for Roanoke Island and for much of the Outer Banks, rivaled only by the boating facilities at Oregon Inlet.

We turned left off the Wanchese road toward the Seafood Park. A couple of more turns and Balls parked near a small building that advertised expert boat repairs and refitting.

"Wait here," Balls said, "or wander around. Don't go too far. I won't be gone long."

I had a good idea what he was up to. Several months earlier I had heard the sheriff ask Balls to check on a couple of brothers down at Wanchese he'd heard rumors might be toying with the idea of trying to bring a load of drugs in from out at sea—meeting a dope-laden boat from one of the islands or South America—and smuggle the goods back to the Outer Banks, maybe even concealed in the bellies of fish. Like some doctors who believe in promoting wellness rather than treating sickness, Sheriff Albright was a big believer in preventive law enforcement when possible. He said he knew it was really a job for DEA, but he felt that Balls' presence, just asking around a bit, might very well make the two brothers reconsider any plans they might be hatching. So maybe what prompted the little private conversation between the sheriff and Balls today meant that this rumor had resurfaced, and time for Balls to mosey around in Wanchese once again.

After sitting in the car for a while, I got out to look at the boats in a yard across the road. What beauties! Some were so large my 18-footer could be towed behind as a dory. I kept glancing back at the Thunderbird in case Balls came out.

When I went back to the car, Balls reappeared in a couple of minutes. The only thing he said for explanation was, "Did a little errand for the good sheriff."

Before he dropped me off at my place we agreed that tomorrow morning I would meet him in the parking lot of Albemarle Hospital in Elizabeth City at nine and we would drive the rest of the way to Rep. Walston's in his car. I would need to leave the house at eight.

As I got out of the car, Balls said, "Keep your eyes open today. One of the deputies will be parked outside tonight." He gave me that grin. "You know you're costing the county a lot of money."

"Look at it this way, Balls. The county's getting me as freebie bait for a murderer."

"Wait a minute," he said. "Get back in the car." He reached under the seat and retrieved a mean looking Python .357 magnum. "Just lending you this temporarily. Don't tell anyone. It's one I carried before we switched to the 9mm."

I took it and hefted its weight. Always surprised how heavy some of the weapons are. "Jeeze. This is a cannon," I said.

"Don't fire it unless you want to knock a hole through an engine block—or somebody. It kicks, too," he said.

I carried the .357 down by my side as I went to my outside stairway and into the house. I laid the gun on the island between the kitchen and living room. It dwarfed the .32 revolver beside it.

Just as dark was coming on, one of the Dare County Sheriff Department vehicles pulled into my cul-de-sac. I went down to speak to the deputy. I didn't know him. We shook hands and I saw his name tag, Dorsey. He looked about twenty-five, crewcut light colored hair, already beginning to thin, and a round face that looked like it hardly needed a razor.

"Can I get you anything?"

"No sir. I'm okay. Got a couple of sandwiches and my wife fixed me a Thermos of coffee. I'll keep a sharp eye out, sir."

I thanked him and told him if there was anything he needed, just let me know.

Some time after I had gone to bed—I think I had just dozed off—I heard the deep-throated engine on Deputy Dorsey's cruiser start up. I got up, slipped on a pair of slacks, took the .357 in my right hand, and opened the kitchen door to the deck just as I saw Dorsey pull rapidly out of the cul-de-sac and turn right toward Kitty Hawk Bay. "Where the hell is he going?" I muttered.

I stood there in the night, which was illuminated by my outside lights, the gun by my side. I was just about to go inside and call the sheriff's office to find out where Dorsey was when headlights coming from the Bypass side turned into my street.

At first I thought it was Dorsey returning.

Then the realization came over me with a chill. It wasn't Dorsey's cruiser.

The dark late model Cadillac glided to a stop at the far end of my driveway. The headlights clicked on and off twice. I cocked the hammer with my thumb, raised the revolver, steadying it with both hands.

The headlights went off, but then the interior dome light came on and I could see him sitting at the wheel. He leaned forward so he could look up at me through his windshield. I couldn't see him plainly, but it looked like he was smiling at me. He waved one hand. The dome light went off, he put the Cadillac in reverse, did a quick three-point turn-around, and he was gone.

The night was cool, but I felt a drop of perspiration run down my side. The wind had shifted to the northeast and was beginning to blow steadily.

I carefully eased the hammer of the revolver back down, and waited.

From the direction of Kitty Hawk Bay, here came the Dare County cruiser, swinging into my street, backing into his spot by the huge live oak.

Deputy Dorsey lowered his window and peered his baby face up at me.

I stalked down the stairs to his cruiser, still holding the .357 by my side. "Deputy, where in the hell have you been?"

"Sir?"

"You're supposed to stay here, damn it."

"Oh, this car came into the street, blinked his lights, and then took off toward the sound. I went after him."

"Please . . . stay here."

"Yes, sir, I will. But I figured . . . well, anyway, whoever it was just plain disappeared, like a ghost. I mean he was gone."

"Well, he came back."

"Huh? Sir?"

"He came back. I'm standing out there on the deck with this gun in my hand."

Dorsey glanced down at the wicked looking cannon in my hand.

More to myself than to Dorsey, I said, "The son of a bitch actually waved at me."

"Sir, I'll stay right here. And I've got my weapon handy. I'm sorry about that. Won't happen again."

"Thanks, Dorsey." The wind whipped the branches of the live oak. Even the scrubby pine tree in the front had begun to sway. "I'm going back inside."

"Goodnight, sir, and don't you worry none."

Yeah, not to worry. Here was this guy who seemed to be able to appear and disappear in an instant. He's watching everything, or seems to be. Knew how to draw the deputy away from the house, lead him on a chase and disappear once again, only to reappear from a different direction.

What's the bastard up to? Other than to try to keep me on edge until he makes some move. And more importantly, *why* is he doing this?

Balls is probably right. He's playing with us, showing us he's in charge and calling the shots. He's having fun.

But ultimately, what's driving him to do this? Is he being paid to do it? Really a hit man? That seems certainly possible, but there's something else, too.

He likes this. He's getting his jollies. It's a power thing, just like beating up Carter Lewiston and using Tracy Keller as a punching bag—until he decides it's time to kill them.

So, who's next? He's not through. I know that.

Chapter Twenty

I was up early. Didn't feel like I'd slept more than a fitful couple of hours. I went down to speak to Dorsey, who tried to appear alert and watchful. I apologized for jumping all over him.

"You were absolutely right, sir. But everything was quiet the rest of the night."

I told him I would be leaving very shortly to drive over to Elizabeth City. He said he would stay right here until I left.

Before I left, I called Balls and told him about last night.

He was quiet. Then he said, "He's still playing. And I don't think it's you that he's after—not yet anyway. Let's face it. He could of made a move on you before now, way that cat's slipping around. At any rate, carry that big gun with you. Wrap it in a towel and put it under the seat."

The drive over to Elizabeth City, which takes about an hour, went smoothly. But I watched every car coming and going. I pulled into the visitor's parking area of Albemarle Hospital a few minutes before nine. Balls was waiting for me.

We drove toward Hertford. Rep. Walston's house was an attractive white frame house, a wide porch that faced the Perquimans River.

Balls parked in the circular drive near the front door. The two-car garage was shut but a small Honda SUV was parked facing the garage. As we started to the front door, Balls said, "We'll both play Mr. Nice Guy—at least to start."

The Congressman's wife, Hilda Walston, opened the front door and smiled a greeting. She was a bit younger than I expected from a picture I had seen. She wore her blondish hair cut short and brushed back, dressed casually in slacks and cotton golf shirt. Trim.

"Hope you had no trouble finding the place," she said as she led us to the left. "Jeremy and Melvin are in the den. Can I get you coffee?"

"That would be fine, Mrs. Walston," Balls said.

I could smell the pleasant aroma of bacon that had been cooked a short time earlier.

Both Melvin and the Congressman stood when Balls and I entered the den, dominated by a huge television set tuned to CNN with the audio muted. Walston had the remote in his right hand and he clicked the TV off and shifted the remote to his left so he could shake hands. He put the remote on a coffee table in front of the leather sofa where Melvin had been sitting. Walston took his seat in an upholstered leather chair that was probably a recliner as well. He was smiling and charming, khaki slacks, open-neck button-down shirt.

A plate with a bite or two of Danish remained on the coffee table in front of Melvin. His bright green sport shirt was too small for him.

I sat on the other end of the sofa so I could see Balls, Walston and Melvin. Hilda came in with the coffee, and took a seat in a chair near Walston.

Walston said, "Now tell me, Agent Twiddy and Mr. Weaver, as the drunk said who got on a crowded elevator facing those already on, 'I guess you wonder why I called this meeting.' And maybe I am too."

Melvin chuckled at the joke, which I'm sure he had heard countless times before. Hilda smiled rather weakly.

"Well, Congressman," Balls said, "as you know, an investigation is ongoing into the slaying of Mr. Carter Lewiston. So we are just trying to track down any reason that he may have been killed. The theory is, of course, that a motive could lead us closer to the perpetrator."

"But that still doesn't tell me why you are here."

"Oh, I think, Congressman, that's pretty obvious. First of all, Carter Lewiston was the secretary-treasurer of this group planning the ethanol plant, for which a grant of three and a quarter million dollars has been approved, and as I understand, a goodly portion of that has been distributed. And secondly, Melvin here mentioned to Mr. Weaver, who also discussed with you, rumors that there were in fact no plans to actually build an ethanol plant."

"Oh, I think that rumor's tommyrot," Walston said, his face beginning to cloud with a trace of anger.

"It may very well be, Congressman, and after talking with Gifford Grudgeon, I'm inclined to believe that plans are being laid to actually build the plant—at least I can see why Grudgeon and some of the others would benefit from actually having the plant."

"Of course there're benefits," Walston said. "This great country of ours shouldn't be so dependent on those . . . those folks in the Middle East. And furthermore—"

"Excuse me, sir, and I can't help but wonder why you suggested to Mr. Weaver here that he visit with Grudgeon to get a list of those involved when you knew all of the players yourself." Balls nodded toward Hilda, "Including good Mrs. Walston."

She spoke up, "Oh, I'm more of a figurehead than anything else. Just so I can keep the Congressman apprised of what's going on."

Walston's face had reddened. With practiced political skill, Walston didn't answer Balls' question directly but said instead, "Now, listen here, Agent Twiddy, I want to be as helpful as possible, but it sounds like to me you're just on some sort of fishing expedition and I'm not sure I like the flow of your line, so to speak."

"No offense intended, Congressman. I'm just in the midst of a real puzzling investigation. We're trying to find out *why* Mr. Lewiston was killed, in hopes that will lead us to *who* killed him."

"I think you're fishing in the wrong pond," Walston said, breathing easier.

Melvin put two pieces of the Danish in his mouth at once. He didn't seem to be able to get comfortable on the sofa.

Balls gave that grin of his. "Tell you the truth, Congressman, I'd surely rather be out fishing Currituck Sound or right here on the Perquimans River than doing this sort of thing. But understand, sir, it's my job and sometimes I have to ask questions I'd rather not ask."

The Congressman appeared to relax in his chair. "I understand," Walston said.

"And here's one of those questions." Balls shifted his gaze to Hilda and back to the Congressman. "Why isn't Steve Partens here? Mrs. Walston's brother. Isn't he now the head of this whole project—especially since your job, Congressman, was to sort of get the grant on a fast-track . . . so to speak, and Mrs. Walston here is just a figurehead, as she says."

Hilda spoke up, "Oh, I'm sorry. I should have mentioned that earlier. Steve is coming. Should be here shortly. I called him and reminded him. He said he had been tied up. He'll be here, though."

No sooner had she finished than the phone rang. She picked up the handset and stepped away from the group to take the call. In a moment she stepped back. "Steve's on the line. He's still tied up over at Albemarle Plantation. You know, that resort community? He wants to know if you can't make it another time."

Balls said, "I know where Albemarle Plantation is. Tell him just to stay there and we'll be there to see him very shortly. Main lobby area."

Hilda looked hesitant, then relayed the message. She clicked the phone off. "He said okay."

He must have said more than that but she didn't repeat it. I saw Hilda and Walston exchange glances, looks that conveyed a message we weren't privileged to.

Chapter Twenty-One

Balls stood and shook hands with the Congressman. "Thank you for your time, sir. I hope you understand that I'm just asking a lot of questions, trying to put pieces of a puzzle together."

"I understand completely. Glad that we could be of help. If you need anything else, just contact me or Melvin here."

Outside, Balls said, "You see that look between Hilda and Mr. Politician?"

"Yeah. They're worried. Something about her brother bothers them both."

"Um-huh, you're right. And we're going to go see Mr. Partens right now before he gets himself 'tied up' someplace else."

The way Balls drove we were there at the gated entrance to Albemarle Plantation in about twenty minutes. It was nestled grandly amidst live oaks and towering pine trees. Balls flashed his badge at the gate attendant and told him we had an appointment at the clubhouse. The attendant waved us through. We wound around immaculate curved paved roads, greenery on both sides, until we pulled up in front of the main entrance to the combination club house, dining room and lobby, with its porch and rocking chairs that stretched across the front of the structure.

The dining room was empty except for an elderly couple near the window and a lone man with a cup of coffee sitting to one side. The man had to be Steve Partens because he looked expectantly at us as we entered, half-smiled, nodded his head as if he didn't have good control over it. He was in his late forties, I guessed, thin, with reddish hair that looked too long for his lean, drawn face. The way he moved and thrust his arm out to shake hands reminded me of one of those old-timey marionettes, all loose-jointed and jerky.

"Steve Partens? I'm SBI Agent Twiddy and this is Harrison Weaver."

Partens nodded his head quickly. I had the impression he couldn't stop its bobbing.

Balls and I took seats at the table. Balls said, "I'm looking into the death of one Mr. Carter Lewiston, who as I understand it was in partnership with you on this ethanol project."

"Well, he was one of several," Partens said, looking around maybe for a waitress. "Want some coffee?"

"Sure."

Partens waved one of his long arms at the middle-age waitress standing to one side near the door to the kitchen. He pointed a finger at his coffee, and then us. He started to pick his cup up but his hand shook so he put the cup back in its saucer, where some of the coffee had spilled.

"That was really bad about Carter," Partens said. "He was a nice man."

"That's what I understand," Balls said, "and that's the reason that this thing is hard to figure out. What I'm trying to piece together is whether there was any connection between the ethanol project, that big grant that you folks received, and what happened to Mr. Lewiston."

"Oh, no sir, I don't think so. I don't think so at all."

"Why do you say that, Mr. Partens?"

"Huh?"

"Why do you say you don't think there's any connection?"

This time he got his coffee cup up to his lips, took a rather loud sip, and said, "I just don't, that's all. I mean, why would there be?" There was a touch of aggressiveness in his tone.

"How much money from the grant have you all received?"

"Now, this is a private business matter. I don't know I'm at liberty to tell you that . . . or whether I have to."

"No, of course you don't *have* to. But these are public funds and the record will be available—if I have to take steps to acquire the figures."

Partens stared at his coffee cup. "A little over a million," he said. He looked around, "Where's the waitress with your coffee?"

Balls said, "I thought it was more like three and a quarter million."

"Oh . . . well, they don't give it to you all at once."

"I see. But I thought that in this case they had. And I also understand there've been some private contributions, also."

The waitress came with the coffee. I asked for a glass of water. She went for the water without saying anything. She brought the water and actually smiled when she set it down.

Partens leaned forward, his arms on the table, head thrust forward so that his shoulders hunched up like folded wings. "Look, I don't know anything about Carter's death. And this ethanol plant is going to get built, and it'll be good for the whole area, and I've really got some business to take care of, and everything, and I don't have time to keep going over this."

"We really haven't gone over it, Mr. Partens. We've just started talking about it."

"Well, but I'm busy. I mean I'm really busy."

Balls stirred his coffee slowly, took a long sip, set the cup down carefully, and leaned forward. "Mr. Partens, I'm concerned, and I think you are too. That killer is still out there."

Partens jerked his head up and down, signaling that he understood.

"We think that he has—in a way—threatened Mr. Weaver here, and he may very well have caused the death of another individual. So, Mr. Partens, if there's something you could tell us that would help unravel this thing, it would be good all the way around. See, from everything we can determine, the only connection for any reason that someone would want to eliminate Carter Lewiston is his involvement in this big ethanol project. And since you're deeply involved in the project, too, I can't help but wonder—and I'm not saying this to cause you any undue worry—just how safe you are."

The color left Partens' face. He pushed his coffee away. "Oh, I'm safe," he said. "Yes, I'm safe."

"Well, Mr. Partens, I don't mean any offense by it, but you seem awfully nervous to me."

"I'm just busy. Really busy. I mean, this is a big project, and it falls on my shoulders now."

I couldn't help but look at those bony shoulders.

Balls pulled out one of his cards and pushed it across the table to Partens. "If you want to talk later, or at any time, just call me, Mr. Partens. Call me on that cell number listed."

"I will. I will. But I've really got to go now." He scraped his chair back from the table. "Don't worry about the coffee. I've got it."

Partens spoke to the waitress as he left, nodding toward our table.

Balls absently stirred what was left of his coffee with a spoon. Then he got a trace of a grin on his face. "You ever see that movie *Fargo*? That actor that played the manager of the car dealership? William H. Macy, or some name like that? All nervous and guilty and all? Well, Partens reminds me of a tall, skinny version of that guy."

I nodded my head, jerkily.

Balls grinned, then got serious. "Mr. Partens here is in deep doggie-doo. I don't know how or why yet, but he's scared. Not just nervous. He's scared too."

When we went outside, to our surprise there was Partens standing in the middle of the walkway with his cell phone to his head. As we approached, he flipped the phone shut. I'm not at all sure he was actually talking to anyone. He may have been just waiting for us.

He hunched his shoulders as if he was cold and said to Balls, "You really think I might be in some kind of danger? I mean not safe or something?"

Balls stared at Partens for several seconds without speaking, his face dead serious. "Is there something you want to tell me, Mr. Partens?"

"No, no. I was just, you know, curious why you said what you said back in there. Just curious."

Balls sighed. "We know that killer is still out there. He seems to have an interest in people like Carter Lewiston and a young woman who was paid to do a phony investigation on Lewiston. They both end up dead. So, yes, I'd suggest you be careful."

"Well, I sure don't know anything about. . . ."

"Yeah, you've told me that." Balls stepped closer to Partens. "I think you need to talk to me."

"No, I've told you everything."

"I beg your pardon, Mr. Partens, but the fact is you haven't told me *anything*. And I think something's eating at you."

"No, no, I'm just busy . . . that's all." He jerked his head up and down a couple of times.

Balls said, "I'll be talking with you some more, Mr. Partens." Then as we started to continue to the car, Balls turned and said once more, "Just be careful, Mr. Partens."

Partens strode away, arms and legs looking loose-jointed like that marionette.

In the car, I said to Balls, "He may remind you of the character in *Fargo*, but he reminds me of the Mad Hatter in *Alice in Wonderland* who's always saying, 'I'm late, I'm late, I'm late.'"

Balls didn't start the engine, just sat there staring straight ahead. "He's not clean. He may not be totally dirty, but he's got himself involved in something. And I think that something might be too big for him."

He turned the ignition on and we started back to Elizabeth City.

Chapter Twenty-Two

That was the last time we saw Steve Partens alive.

He was fished out of the Perquimans River late Sunday afternoon with two small bullet holes behind his left ear. The medical team estimated he had been in the river since late Saturday night or in the early hours of Sunday.

Balls called me at home about six o'clock Sunday evening to tell me about it.

I felt a chill of dread. I said, "Jesus, what the hell is going on?"

"You know what's going on. The son of a bitch is eliminating anyone with a connection to him . . . and Mr. Partens did have a connection."

My voice didn't sound quite normal as I said, "You sound sure of that, the connection I mean."

"I am." He paused as if thinking over how much he should tell me. "Partens called me last night."

I was surprised. "He did?"

"Actually, I kind of figured he would. I knew he had something on his chest when we were there with him yesterday, and he was scared. Had a right to be."

"God, dead, just like that." My breathing was shallow.

"Yeah, two bullets to the head will usually do that."

I tried to take it logically. "What'd he tell you?"

"Started off by getting ready to say he didn't really know anything but—and I interrupted him and told him to cut out the bullshit. I said you called me because you *do* know something.

Then he said, 'Mother of God forgive me, but I might have played a part in how this whole thing started. Didn't mean to but, oh God, I might have.' I said tell me about it, Mr. Partens, trying to be patient with him, not scare him off. He said, 'Not over this cell phone. Meet me in the morning at Albemarle Plantation, breakfast time, eight-thirty, nine latest.' I said I'd be there—but our poor Mr. Partens didn't make it all the way through the night."

I said, "When you got there, and he didn't show. . . ."

"That's when I figured something not too pleasant had happened to him. Initiated a search for him. By chance two guys out boating spotted him there in the river late this afternoon."

"Then you think maybe he's the one somehow got this son of a bitch started, then the guy turns on him? Not sure that makes sense," I said.

"Why not? Maybe the guy milked all he could out of it, then gets rid of the competition."

"What about Hilda and Congressman Walston? Think they knew, or involved?"

He was silent. I could hear him breathing because he held the mouthpiece close to his face. Then he said, "Could be. Not sure how clean they are. I got the feeling yesterday when we were ready to leave, and they exchanged those looks, that maybe they suspected Brother Steve was in over his head. At the very least I get a feeling they suspected that. And I believe they were worried about how stable Partens was." He paused again. "I'll be going over there shortly."

Balls breathed out a long sigh. Then he said, "You heard what I said earlier? You know, eliminating those who have any connection?"

"Yes, I heard." I tried to sound normal.

"Well, you may be the only one left with a connection to him."

"You don't need to remind me. I know."

"I want you to really watch your backside. Sleep with that big gun. I'm going to make sure there's a deputy over there, maybe even twenty-four-seven. I'll check see whether Odell Wright is on duty. He's good."

While he talked, I turned on the outside lights, even though it wasn't even dusk yet. Damn right I was going to watch my backside. I eyed the .357 that lay reassuringly close at hand on the divider between the kitchen and the living room.

After we hung up, I sat very still in the chair by the phone. I could feel those little beads of perspiration, cool against my side.

Odell Wright was the deputy assigned. When he arrived, with dusk coming on, he blinked his lights twice. I went down to greet him. "I'm glad you are here, Odell."

Odell said, "We're going to get that bastard before he does anymore damage."

I wished I shared Odell's optimism.

No trouble during the night and Monday morning was bright and almost cloudless. Temperature already promising a warm and pleasant day. Murder seemed almost impossible on days like this.

I took Odell fresh coffee. While we chatted, another deputy drove up in a regular Dare County Sheriff's Department car. He took up position by the live oak. It was a deputy I had seen around the courthouse but didn't know personally.

I told the new deputy to come on in the house at any time to use the bathroom or get something to eat. As I went back up the stairs I thought, hell, how long is this going to go on?

Twice during the day the deputy came up to use the bathroom and visited for a few minutes before he went back down to his cruiser.

It was late in the afternoon before I heard from Balls again.

He said, "Everything been quiet today?"

"Yes. I've stayed here all day, actually getting some work done."

"I've got news," he said.

"Yeah? You caught the bastard?"

"Yeah, don't we wish. But I got a good lead on how he has been financed. Half the three mil is gone from the account—allegedly for another 'feasibility' study. I think it is money that

Partens gave to our mystery man, gave it to him maybe because he was being threatened. Too much for a regular payoff for a hit man. I think Partens was trying to buy his own safety."

"Didn't work," I said.

"I got a feeling Partens didn't know or realize in the beginning that he was dealing with a perp who just likes killing. It's a game to him. That's how Partens got in over his head."

"What about the good Congressman and his wife?"

"I don't know. Saw them last night, expressed condolences and all that sort of thing. But asked a lot of questions, too. They're still being pretty slick. I believe they suspected something. But involved directly? I don't know."

"Somebody had to put Partens in touch with this guy, this killer. And the killer's certainly no amateur."

Again he paused. "That's a main reason I keep you filled in. This guy's no amateur, and . . . well, just let me or the sheriff or Odell or somebody know where you are and where you're going at all times."

"Jesus, Balls, I can't live my life cooped up here in this little house." I forced a chuckle. "Although I am getting a lot of work done. Book is right on deadline."

"Screw the book. You got your ass to worry about."

"I'll definitely keep you posted. But if the weather holds, I might just get out, go get something to eat, enjoy being here at the Outer Banks."

"Call first." Then he said, "After tonight, we may just have the deputies parked there at your place at night. Cruise by during the day, but twenty-four seven may not be necessary."

"I don't think it is," I said. "During the day I'll have that big gun with me and I'll be on the lookout."

We rang off. Elly had been on my mind, despite all of the pressure from the investigation, not to mention potential danger. I called her. "It's Harrison," I said.

"Oh, yes. I remember you."

"Don't be a smarty."

"Just trying to keep things a bit light," she said, and the word "light" came out softly as "loight." Then she said, "Any progress you can tell me about? And much more important, are you doing what you should be doing to stay safe?"

"First question, very little progress, so it's not a matter of whether I can tell you or not. Just ain't much to tell."

"I heard about the Congressman's brother-in-law. It was on the news last evening. Didn't you go to see him."

"Briefly."

"That's what worries me. You are too close to all of this."

"Other part of your question . . . I've got a deputy sheriff sitting out there right now in a cruiser keeping an eye out, and another will be there all night."

"I feel better with someone there."

"I think Balls wants someone here at least at night until this thing is settled."

She was quiet a moment. "I miss you," she said.

"I miss you, too, Elly. I'll be glad when this is over, too. I'm ready for us to, you know, get back to a normal life like we should have."

"Me, too, Harrison."

"But right now, I don't think it's wise for me to be around you. I don't want to get you involved or put you close to, to this situation."

She huffed out a slightly mocking, "*Situation*? That what you call it? You're dealing with a killer that acts like a psycho or something. That's more than a situation."

We talked a bit longer. I asked how Martin was, and her mother. Then I said, "I'll call you tomorrow evening."

"No," she said. "Call me in the morning before I go to work. I want to know you had a safe night and good sleep."

"You're wonderful. I'll call. Promise."

As dark was beginning to come on, Odell called to say he was driving up to relieve the other deputy. In less than a minute he pulled into the cul-de-sac and blinked his lights twice. I went down stairs to thank the deputy who was leaving and to say hello to Odell.

Later that night I tried watching television, surfing about, not staying on any one program long. Close to nine-thirty the phone rang. I looked at it from across the room as if it were something offensive. And it probably was.

The caller ID was blocked.

I picked up the handset. "Yes?"

The syrupy Southern accent: "Now, buddy boy, are you going to live the rest of your life with armed guards watching your—pardon the language—watching your ass every minute? That's no way to live." He sighed. "Might as well be dead."

"Listen, you son of a bitch—"

"Now, there you go again, calling me vile names, when after all, I might really be your best friend, so to speak." He chuckled. "After all, you're still alive, aren't you?"

He clicked off.

I immediately called Balls and told him.

"Damn," he said. "We should have set up a monitoring device for your telephone right from the beginning. He may be blocking caller ID but if he stays on that phone long enough we could track him."

"He was on less than a minute."

I could hear the exasperation in his voice: "Shit."

"Me, too," I said. "Shit." The catchall word when things have gone steadily downhill, or when disaster is at hand.

Janey chirped and then said as clear as a bell, "Shit."

I realized she should have been covered up for bedtime an hour ago. I checked her seeds and water, gave her a tiny bit of millet, and covered her cage.

Screw it, I thought. Tomorrow, goddamn it, I'm going out, get some coffee, at least look at the ocean and pay my respects to it, maybe stop for lunch. I'll take the big gun with me but I'll be damn if I'm going to be held hostage by that bastard.

Chapter Twenty-Three

After I brought Odell fresh coffee the next morning, I went back in to take a shower. When I came out of the bathroom, I looked out the kitchen door. Odell had left. He had put the empty coffee cup on the steps. I called Elly before she left for work and told her everything was fine. I got dressed in khakis, golf shirt and boat shoes, no socks. Outer Banks dressy attire. I had decided to go down to Good Life Gourmet for one of their specialty coffees and a Danish, maybe bring a couple of them home. I tried to figure out how I could carry the .357 into the restaurant with me. Gave up on it. Too bulky. I figured I'd leave it under the front seat, wrapped in the towel, lock the car.

A bright sunny day again, light wind from the southwest, maybe just a touch of humidity that I figured would build during the day. But for now, the morning was crisp and new and murder and danger seemed to have receded from the world.

The restaurant was not crowded, which pleased me. I placed an order for a Danish I pointed to and paid for it and a coffee, helping myself from one of the three urns on a counter. I got a Kenyan blend, rich and full-bodied. A retirement-age couple I'd seen before sat at one of the tables in the middle. Two women were in a booth toward the rear with brochures of houses spread on the table between them, apparently talking real estate. I took a seat at one of the small tables against the wall, with a view toward the large plate glass window and the main counter to my right. One of the servers, a young woman who still appeared sleepy, brought my Danish. I told her to make it two more to go. I think better with a little sugar fix. At least I think I do. A lanky young man who reminded me of a youthful Steve Partens came in with his laptop and set it up two tables in front of me. The café has wireless so he tapped into the Internet almost as soon as he sat down. Out of the corner of my eye I saw another couple come in, and then a lone man with a scraggly beard, ratty sneakers and jeans, wearing an "Awful Arthur's" T-shirt and a greasy baseball cap, went back toward the counter behind me. I heard him tell the young server in a flat North Carolina accent, "Jes' coffee."

It was good to be out.

I took my time, refilled my half-empty coffee cup once.

The elderly couple got up, moving slowly, and left. Then the man with the scraggly beard, jeans, and ratty sneakers sauntered toward the front and followed the elderly couple out. There was something about the way the bearded guy walked, the relaxed casual stroll that seemed somehow vaguely familiar, tugging at my memory. It was a different walk, I sensed, than when he came in.

Aw, Christ, I thought. I'm getting paranoid. Yet. . . .

Less than a minute later, the dark late model Cadillac pulled up to the curb, the driver's side facing the plate glass window. Oh, shit, it was the guy. He had removed his greasy baseball cap, smoothed down his sandy-colored hair. He looked in at me, a half-smile on his face, and with one motion, whipped off the false scraggly beard. He gave a casual salute, gunned the Cadillac and whipped it toward the Bypass. He was gone before I could get to the front door of the café.

"Be right back," I called to the woman behind the counter. I raced to my car, unlocked the door and grabbed my cell phone. I dialed the sheriff's office. I was hoping that Mabel was dispatcher, but she wasn't. The call was answered by a male I didn't recognize.

"This is Harrison Weaver. I'm in the Dare Centre in Kill Devil Hills. There's a late model Cadillac headed south, I think, on the Bypass. He needs to be stopped for questioning. Connection with a couple of killings, Carter Lewiston."

"Who is this, sir?"

"Harrison Weaver, a friend of SBI Agent Twiddy's—and the sheriff."

"Are you with the SBI?"

"No. But I know the driver needs to be stopped."

"Did you get his license number, sir?"

"No . . . Listen, just send someone looking for him."

"Well, sir, you're not an officer and there are a lot of Cadillacs out there, and—"

"Okay, okay. Just forget it. He's gone now anyway."

"Well, sir—"

"Goodbye."

I knew I needed to call Balls. I got his answering machine. I clicked off, picked up the towel-wrapped .357 and put it under my arm, locked the car, and went slowly back in Good Life Gourmet, cell phone in my pocket. As I reached the door, my phone rang. Standing outside, I flipped it on.

"You called me," Balls said.

I told him what had happened.

"Oh, he's having a friggin' ball, isn't he?" Balls said. "I'll call and find out who that dipshit dispatcher is. I wish to hell you'd get back home and stay there."

"Damn it, Balls, I'm not going to spend my life holed up somewhere."

"Yeah, that sounds tough. But that's assuming you got some life left in you"

I went back inside Good Life Gourmet to take one last sip of my now cold coffee, picked up my bag with the Danish and paid for them, and then despite the bravado I had expressed to Balls, I returned to my house, and locked the door.

The next day went along without incident—until mid-afternoon when I got a call from Elly. She was calling from work and I could tell from her tone right off the bat that she was distraught.

"Maybe it's nothing, Harrison. But it worries me."

"What?"

"I just got a call from Mother." She took in a breath. "She said she had to call Martin and Lauren, the little girl next door, into the house. They were outside, just down the street a little ways, standing along the edge of the road when a car pulled up." She paused and I heard her trying to control her voice and talk slowly. "Mother happened to look out the window and it appeared that whoever was in the car was talking to the children. Mother didn't like it, and she went out on the porch and called to Martin and Lauren and told them to come back home that instant."

I gripped the phone tightly.

"The two of them came back to the house and the car drove away. She asked Martin what the driver was saying to them." She took another deep breath. "You know how Martin is. He doesn't talk much but he said the man asked them if they'd like to go for a ride." There was almost a sob in her voice. "Lauren said the man was real nice."

"I'll bet he was," I mumbled.

"It scared me, Harrison," she said. "It still does."

I almost hesitated to ask. "What kind of car was it?"

"Mother didn't know. She said it was a big car, not an SUV." She took another breath before she said, "And it was dark-colored."

Hardly realizing I had spoken, I whispered, "Oh, shit." Then I said, "I'll call Sheriff Albright and report it to him. I know he'll have a deputy patrolling near your place."

"I've already told Mabel and she said she'd tell the sheriff and make sure they're on the lookout."

She paused and I knew she weighed her words. "Harrison, it's bad enough that you are in danger, but I can't have . . . well, I just can't have it."

"I understand. It may not be anything. Really, it might not." Then I said, "But keep Martin close."

"Don't worry." There was crispness in her voice, a distancing from me that I could feel and understand.

When we hung up, I muttered to myself, "Okay, you bastard, you've gone too far. I'm going to get you. I'm going to get you, you slimy son of a bitch."

• • •

The rest of the day was quiet. Of course I couldn't get the thought out of my mind that I might be putting Elly and her son in danger. But maybe the son of a bitch was just playing more of his games, letting us know he was in control. Then, too, it's possible that this was someone else, another pedophile, or maybe it was nothing at all. Yeah, right.

A deputy drove into the cul-de-sac two or three times that afternoon. One would be parked outside at night. This constant surveillance and protection was putting a strain on the department's resources, I knew, and I didn't think it could reasonably be kept up much longer. But Balls said the sheriff was justifying it because their best chance of catching the killer was when he came after me. Yeah, doesn't that make me feel great.

Late that evening I called Elly. A worry was still in her tone. She said she was keeping Martin in the house the next day "until this thing gets settled." Trying to change the subject and put her more at ease, I suggested I come to see her on Saturday, maybe go out to eat. She said we could stay at the house and she would fix something. She said that might be more sensible.

I also talked with Balls, listened to his frustration that nothing was happening. He went to Steve Partens' funeral on Thursday, keeping an eye out, he said. He said he had a long talk with the Congressman and Hilda who were down for the funeral in nearby Tyrrell County, where Partens was born. "I'm convinced that they know more than they're letting on," he said.

"About the ethanol project?"

"Indirectly, yeah. You know Partens told me he might have played a part in setting this thing in motion. Well, yeah, but I think maybe the first little nudge might have come from somewhere else, maybe either the Congressman or his sweet wife."

I waited. Balls didn't continue, so I said, "Don't leave me hanging."

"Maybe Hilda or Walston didn't contact our mystery man, but I think he or she probably knew someone who could."

"That's heavy stuff, Balls."

"Yeah, I know it, and I got to be real careful with it. Only reason I'm telling you is, well, you know why."

"You don't think he's through with me?"

"Nope."

"But why would the Congressman, in his position, get involved with a goddamn killer?"

"My thought is that he—or she—didn't know they were. I think maybe, and I'm just putting pieces together here, that Carter Lewiston was making noises about pulling out because he thought something was fishy, and Hilda, or the Congressman, talked to someone who they believed could put a little pressure on Lewiston to make him shut up, and stick with them. Not do him in, but keep him quiet."

"You're putting a whole lot of pieces of puzzle together, Balls, it seems to me, and you might be forcing it a bit."

"Of course I'm forcing it. Shit, I don't have anything else."

"No offense." Then I said, "I've got something else to tell you. It may not be anything, but it worries me and it sure as hell worries Elly Pedersen." I related the incident.

When I finished, Balls was quiet. "Of course it may not be anything. But wouldn't put it past the guy. Another way of tormenting, playing his power game. I'll check with the sheriff, see if there've been any other recent incidents like this." He gave a short laugh. "For once, I hope there is some weirdo out there in a dark car trying to pick up kids . . . and this thing not related to our bastard."

We clicked off and it wasn't thirty minutes later that Balls called back. As soon as I answered, he said, "Forget the late model Cadillac."

"Huh?"

"One was found abandoned in the parking lot at the theater complex there in Kill Devil Hills. Turns out it was stolen over a month ago in Fairfax, Virginia, equipped with stolen Pennsylvania tags. Wiped clean of any prints, you can bank on that. I'll still get a team go over it. So now our man is driving something else—and we don't know what. And he may have been driving something else today. I expect, though, another report of a stolen vehicle will turn up, unless he went up the street and bought himself a legitimate one. We'll be checking out both angles."

"This doesn't make me feel any easier," I said. "But in a way it may make Elly feel better."

"Oh, and guess who got suspicious about the Cadillac? Your young Deputy Dorsey, the one you chewed out for driving off the other night."

"He's redeemed himself."

Friday morning I got another surprise. Shortly after the deputy left, here came a fairly new Toyota Camry with Virginia tags pulling into my cul-de-sac. I picked up the .357, held it by my side and eased open the door to the deck.

The Camry's door opened and Melvin Mellencamp squeezed out from behind the wheel, looking at my house number, then seeing me, he waved.

Chapter Twenty-Four

Melvin appeared to have gained more weight since last Saturday. He waddled up the outside stairs, and was puffing a bit when he got to the top. He eyed the .357 I'd shifted to my left hand, down by my side. He cocked his head, "Expecting *bad* company?"

"Never know. What are you doing at the Outer Banks? And this early in the morning?"

"Taking an extra long weekend. I came down last night. Didn't go to the funeral. Staying over at the Hilton Gardens. Heck, got an ocean view, too."

"Your mother lives over on the mainland at East Lake, doesn't she? Thought you'd stay there."

"No, thought I'd live it up a little. Besides, as I told you, she works part-time over at one of the gift shops on Festival Park in Manteo. I'll see her plenty."

I ushered him in. "How'd you find my place?" I laid the revolver on the counter and pushed it back against the wall.

"Not that complicated," he said. "You go up the beach or down the beach. That's about it. And besides, you gave me one of your cards when you were up there for Tracy's service."

He said "Tracy's service" as casually as he might have mentioned he went to a cocktail party.

I started another pot of coffee, and had some left over Danish which Melvin accepted when I nodded toward it.

He looked up at me. "I'm going back with Hand Gun Restriction. Left the Congressman. Got a few days off."

"Why'd you leave Walston? I thought you were his right hand man, chief of staff."

"That's what I wanted to talk to you about. But it's got to be real confidential. Kept quiet."

"Shit, Melvin, everything you tell me has to be 'kept quiet.' So why are you telling me?"

"Because I know you want to get the person who did that to Tracy and the two others."

"We don't know for a fact that all three are linked."

"Bullshit. You know they are."

Every now and then Melvin's more assertive nature came out. I heard the coffeepot making the gurgling sound that signaled it had finished.

"Thanks. Cream and sugar if you've got it. Nice cello," he said.

Over my shoulder I said, "It's a bass. Contrabass, bass fiddle, upright bass, string bass. Take your pick. Cello is about half the size."

When I came in with the coffee he had a finger poked in Janey's cage. She eyed him with what appeared to be suspicion.

"Why did you leave the Congressman?"

He stirred his coffee, staring at the cup before he answered. "I think he and his wife, Hilda, know more about how this thing got started than he's letting on."

"What makes you say that?" I thought about what Steve Partens had told Balls, that he felt like he may have helped get it all started. How many hands are in this?

"Now, believe me, I don't think Congressman Walston, or Hilda, thought it would get out of hand like it has. But I don't think they have come clean as to . . . well, how it got started."

"Tell me what you think—and why."

He took a noisy sip of coffee, a bite of the Danish. "Good Danish," he said. "Coffee, too."

I got up and brought him a section of paper towel as a napkin.

He licked one finger, wiped it with the paper towel, and said, "To start with, I think what my mother heard Carter Lewiston say about not building the ethanol plant is in error. Or maybe her interpretation of it was. I think what Lewiston suspected was that Partens or somebody was skimming off the grant money and putting it in his pocket."

I thought about the more than a million that was missing.

Melvin said, "I believe Partens got scared, went to his sister and said that Lewiston was talking and he needed to be quiet. Now, I'm just speculating on a lot of this, you have to understand. That's why I want you to keep it under your hat— at least for the time being. Well, anyway, I suspect that Hilda talked with the Congressman about the situation and how Lewiston could create a scandal, whether it was true or not."

Janey hung upside down in her cage, showing off.

"You know that Walston is real polished, puts on a good front. But he was raised dirt poor and ran with a really rough crowd until he decided to clean up his act and be a politician. But he still knows a bunch of the crowd he grew up with, and some of them are pretty unsavory. He's told me this himself."

"So?"

"There were a few things said between them on Sunday morning as they got ready to go back to Washington—this was before they found Partens or even knew anything had happened to him—that made me begin to put two and two together. It was like they were talking in code, but a word here, word there, and I began to figure it out."

"Well, Christ, Melvin, tell me."

"I think Walston, at probably Hilda's urging, spoke to one of his old cronies back in the county, telling him there was someone who needed to be reminded not to be running his mouth. I don't think the person Walston spoke to is the one directly responsible. But I believe he told Walston it would be taken care of, that he knew someone who could handle just such a job. Walston didn't pay anyone off in money, but he's in a position to, you know, do favors, and I believe that was the pay for the good ol' boy he contacted."

"You're doing a whole lot of speculating, it seems to me, Melvin, and telling me stuff that maybe you ought to be telling the SBI."

"I know your interest in this. And maybe I'm not speculating as much as you think," Melvin said, that assertiveness
surfacing again. "I've taken phone calls for the Congressman, a
guy leaving messages that, when put with other things, make
me pretty sure of what I'm saying. Not one hundred percent, of
course, but . . . you know."

"So what's the payoff for this other guy, the guy the good
ol' boy contacts?"

"I think he shared in the skimming off, or he skimmed it
all off himself, maybe blackmailing Partens." He wiped his
fingers again. "You got any more of that Danish?"

I brought him the other half I had thought about saving for
myself.

"Thanks. Aren't you having any?"

I said, "So, what you're saying about the Congressman and
Hilda is that—"

"They're semi-clean. That make any sense? I don't think
they thought anything like this would happen."

"So why have you left him?"

"He's not being honest about it. I think he knows the guy
he contacted knows this psycho who's doing the killing.
Walston figures he's in a hell of fix. If he 'fesses up, the good
ol' boy says the Congressman put him up to it and then the shit
hits the fan for Walston. He becomes involved in a big scandal,
maybe a trial and he's ruined. Frankly, I don't think he knows
what to do."

"I can tell you what *you* can't do, Melvin. You can't sit on
this."

"That's the reason I'm telling you."

"Hell, I'm not an investigator, Melvin. On the one hand
you tell me to keep a lid on it and then you hand me this stuff
and expect *me* to sit on it?"

"You've got that friend in the SBI, Agent Twiddy. Maybe
he needs to put some pressure on Walston, or Hilda."

I thought about it a minute. "I'll certainly talk to Agent
Twiddy. Tell him what you suspect. It's his investigation. Not
mine."

"Yeah, but you're close to it. Don't try to bullshit me about that, Mr. Weaver."

I stared at him. But he smiled.

He stood, patted his stomach. "Thanks for the Danish and the coffee. I think I'm going to go take in the beach a while."

"Good day for it."

Melvin stopped at the counter, nodded at the .357. "That's a nice Python. Powerhouse. Don't see many of them anymore."

"You know your weapons."

"Well, I guess I should. Hand Gun Restriction for one thing. I've studied handguns a bit. Used to shoot. Target practice, that sort of thing."

Melvin seemed a bit more multifaceted than I'd thought at first.

We stepped out on the deck. "Real good looking boat," he said. "Go out much."

"Haven't been for a while. Need to exercise the motor."

"Yamaha 115. That's a good engine, too."

"Come on back down and we'll go out," I said, with the same sincerity we in the South say, "Y'all come see us, ya hear."

"Well, I'll be back down next week I think. Maybe we can go out then."

"I thought you were going to work for Hand Gun?"

"Oh, I don't start for a while yet." He sucked on a tooth. The Danish, I guessed. "Going to get me a boat one of these days." He chuckled, "But first I want to get me a real nice car."

"You got a good one, that Camry."

"No, I mean something fancy. A Beemer, Audi, or maybe a big-ass Cadillac." He started down the steps, taking them as if his knees hurt. "I'll be real interested in what Agent Twiddy finds out."

"We may never know," I lied. "He has to keep things close to his chest."

I watched him drive away. Janey chirped when I entered, then said the one other word she knows, "Bitch."

Maybe it was the mention of Tracy's memorial service and Hand Gun Restriction, or maybe it was something tugging at my subconscious, but I thought I should call Jean Clayborne to see how she and the others who worked with Tracy were holding up.

I got her right away.

"Good to hear from you, Weav. Envy you down at the Outer Banks, especially on pretty days like this."

We chatted a few minutes and then I mentioned that Melvin Mellencamp had stopped by and that he said he would be joining them again very soon.

"Really? I hadn't heard that. Thought he had that hotshot job on the Hill. Wait a second, Sarah's right here. Let me ask her if she knew this." The conversation at her end was muffled, then Jean came back on. "Sarah doesn't know anything about it. She's handling human relations now. Hold on again." More muffled conversation. "Weav?"

"Yeah?"

"Sarah said she heard Melvin got canned. The Congressman fired him."

Chapter Twenty-Five

Maybe Melvin was too embarrassed to admit he was fired and that he didn't have a job with Hand Gun. But just the same, he lied to me. I didn't like that. Maybe, too, his whole conversation about the involvement of Walston and Hilda was his way of getting back at the Congressman for being fired. Yet, there definitely could be something to what he was saying, and Balls has had the same feeling. I knew I had to relay to Balls everything that Melvin had told me.

To help clear my mind, I tightened and rosined my bow, picked up the bass, checked the tuning and began very slowly playing major scales with no vibrato, using full bow from the frog to the tip, listening carefully to the intonation. Very tricky in the upper ranges. Janey always loves what she must perceive as commotion and chirps happily. I was careful not to say "shit" or "bitch" when my playing was off so she wouldn't keep repeating those two words.

I practiced for twenty minutes or more but I couldn't really concentrate on the playing. Unsorted thoughts about this entire investigation kept tumbling around in the back of my head, never quite coming to the surface. Among things that tugged at my mind, making me feel vaguely uncomfortable was the surprise visit by Melvin Mellencamp. His explanation for why he was telling me what he did made sense. But I wished he hadn't lied about his job situation.

I laid the bass down on its side in the middle of the living room floor, stepped over the neck to get to the phone. I called Balls' cell number.

"We need to talk," I said. I gave him a quick and dirty summation of what Melvin said he suspected.

"Meet me at Sheriff Albright's office in thirty minutes. I'm in Wanchese now. Keep your eyes open—but not necessarily for a Cadillac. Always be equipped."

I wrapped the .357 in its towel and put it just under the front seat of the Saab between my knees.

I pushed the speed a bit more than I like to but I got there in time to stick my head in at the Register of Deeds and say hello to Elly—and to the other two women there in the office with her. I had the feeling that my attention to Elly, and her reciprocating it, provided a bit of spice in the lives of the two women.

Upstairs, I met Mabel as she shuffled back to her small desk. She smiled and nodded toward the sheriff's closed door. "Go on in," she said. "Agent Twiddy and the sheriff are expecting you."

I tapped on the door and entered. Balls slouched in a chair at the far end of the sheriff's desk. Albright gave a half-hearted smile and pointed to a chair. Balls had apparently begun filling in the sheriff on Congressman Walston and Hilda.

Albright shook his massive head. "Oh my, Ballsford, that's awfully, awfully disturbing. I mean, the Right Honorable Jeremy J. Walston, his wife, Hilda. My lord, man, don't even breathe those suspicions outside of this room."

Balls said, "Suspicions might be too strong a word, sheriff. I know that's what I've hinted around at, but I do know that they're worried. Now it may be that they are worried that Brother Steve's involvement—and I don't think there's any question about that—might taint them." Balls nodded toward me. "But let Weav tell you what Walston's staffer, or former staffer, told him today."

I went into detail about Melvin's conversation with me today and how he suspected Walston and his wife were involved, if indirectly, in getting the killings started. When I finished, though, I said, "But I must confess, and Lord knows Balls here is the expert, that for some reason I just have a hard time believing that Walston and his wife somehow set this whole chain of events in motion. I do believe they suspected Steve Partens was in over his head, and maybe doing something unlawful, like skimming off part of the money . . . and now half of it's gone, but where is it?" I turned to Balls. "I'm sure you've been busy checking Partens' financials, probably Walston's too. Found anything?"

Balls shook his head.

"So where's the money?" I said.

"It'll show up," Balls said. "Somewhere. And maybe the killer has it all."

Albright spoke to me. "Your gut feeling is that Walston isn't that much involved?"

"It just doesn't seem likely. It's like it's, I don't know, too obvious that he is, and with Melvin pointing his finger at him. I don't know. Gut feeling, I'll admit." I looked at Balls. "Apologize if I'm talking out of turn. I mean I'm a writer, not a—"

"Yeah, yeah, I know. Not an investigator. But you're the only one we know of—still alive—who has seen the guy we're certain is the perp. And you're in the midst of it because of that. And I have to admit you got good instincts, too."

Albright shook his head again sadly. "So where do we go from here? What's next?"

Balls sighed and sat up straighter in his chair. "I've got to keep looking for the money, and it also looks like I'm going to have to make a trip up to the Washington cesspool to maybe lean just a little more heavily on the good Congressman. Or maybe he'll be coming back to the district in the next few days so I can get him and his wife in the same room, shake it a bit, see what falls out."

I looked from one to the other. I figured they were through with me.

Balls said, "Yeah, you can take off. Be damn careful though. I'm going to be around here a while. I'll check with you later."

I shook hands with the sheriff and left. Downstairs I spoke again to Elly.

She stepped out into the hall. "Everything all right?"

"A standstill. Looking forward to seeing you tomorrow night and not thinking about this . . . this anymore."

She put her fingertips on my arm. "Come over about six, or earlier. It'll be nice."

"I know it will," I said, and meant every word of it.

Traffic was a bit slow getting out of the increasingly up-scale little downtown of Manteo, and it slowed again on 64, the road that would lead me toward the beach. A family in a van with New Jersey tags was in front of me, obviously searching for something because the driver proceeded unsurely, touching his brakes from time to time. I tried not to be exasperated. I glanced around me the whole time, keeping an eye out.

As I approached Manteo Marine on my left, who would be out there waddling around looking at the Hydra-Sport boats but none other than Melvin Mellencamp. I saw his Camry parked off the edge of the road beside the building. Melvin, who was rared back, hands in his pockets, acting expansive, I thought, had the attention of the young salesman.

I thought about pulling over to speak to him, but I didn't stop and after passing McDonald's traffic speed picked up.

For a guy who just got canned from one job and doesn't have the one he claimed to have, ol' Melvin appeared to be acting like the big spender from the East.

When I got to my place, I backed into the driveway, taking a cue from Balls. Upstairs I checked my little bulletin board in the kitchen. A notice I'd clipped from *The Coastland Times* reminded me that a chamber orchestra from the North Carolina School of the Performing Arts was appearing tonight at the Roanoke Island Festival Park in Manteo. Among the pieces they were playing was a selection from Mozart's *Requiem*. I wanted to see if the bass player could perform the section I'd worked on over and over that required crossing the strings repeatedly. That was the piece I'd struggled with, vocally cussing Mozart the whole time, which had, in time, taught Janey to say her choice words.

What the hell. I would go there tonight by myself. There would be enough people around that I would certainly feel safe. Just the same, I called Balls and told him.

"I can't make you stay home," he said. "Take that big gun with you. You'll have on a windbreaker. Stick it in your belt."

That afternoon I got more work done on the book. I sent an email to the editor giving her an update, letting her know I was making the deadline.

It was still light when I left to go over to Festival Park. The performance would start at seven-thirty and I wanted to give myself plenty of time. I crossed the little bridge from downtown Manteo to the park, found a spot for my car under one of the lamps in the parking lot, close to the road. I backed into the space. I was a good forty-five minutes early and decided to browse around the shops and museum.

By chance I saw the gift shop Melvin had mentioned his mother worked in. It was not busy and I strolled in. The lone woman behind the counter smiled. She had to be Melvin's mother. She was a somewhat slimmer version of Melvin but had the same round face.

"Hi, I'm Harrison Weaver, a friend of Melvin's. You Mrs. Mellencamp?"

"Yes indeed," she said. "Melvin's down here for a week, as a matter of fact."

A week? But I said, "Yes, I saw him earlier today. He stopped by the house."

"Oh, you're a local?"

"Am now. Been living here a year and a half. I knew Melvin up in Washington."

"Small world, isn't it? Melvin may come by tonight help me close up."

I'm not sure why I said what came out of my mouth next, but I believe the subconscious does direct us quite often. I said, "I was sorry to hear about your friend Carter Lewiston."

"Huh? Oh, yes, that was a shame. But Mr. Lewiston was not a friend of mine. I used to listen to him on the radio, especially on Sundays, but I never even met him. Sorry I didn't. I hear he was a real nice man. I tell you, doesn't look like any-one's safe anymore. The way this country is going."

I was taken aback. "Oh, I'm sorry. I thought he was a friend of yours." I clearly remembered Melvin had claimed it was his mother—a "real close friend of Carter Lewiston's"—who told him about Lewiston's suspicions concerning the ethanol project.

She shook her head. "I guess I was one of his fans, though. You here for the concert?"

So, another lie from Melvin. But why?

I strolled toward the outdoor concert shell and thought about simply sitting on the grass to listen like so many do. But I thought about that .357 in my belt and knew that would be rather uncomfortable, so I went back to the Saab and got the small folding canvas chair I carried in the trunk.

I got up close to the stage at the side I knew the bass player would be on.

When the music started, I tried to concentrate on it, but my mind kept going over a jumble of mixed up thoughts about this investigation, an investigation that appeared to be going now-here, and the thorny little pieces that jabbed at my conscious-ness.

Chapter Twenty-Six

When the chamber group got to the Mozart piece, I was able to concentrate on the music, or more specifically on the bass player. He was a tall lanky young man and the fingers of his left hand arched expertly over the strings. He used a French bow that he held lightly, almost casually, in his right hand and moved it flawlessly from one string to the other. The son of a bitch didn't even break out in a sweat playing that passage. He had a satisfied smile on his face when they finished. I applauded, even though I hated the bastard.

At the end of the concert, I went up to the bass player and told him I had enjoyed the music. He was very cordial and thanked me. Then I asked him about the section in Mozart's *Requiem*. I told him I had been trying to master it. He laughed and said, "You, too? I worked on that for hours." He added, "I did a lot of fuming and cussing while I was learning it."

So I wasn't the only one. Made me feel better.

The crowd had thinned out considerably by the time I got to my car. I put the fold-up chair back in the trunk. The .357 went back under the front seat. I was glad to get it out of my belt. I kept careful watch on everyone around me, the drivers, other cars, as well as the pedestrians. Everything went smoothly. I reached my street in Kill Devil Hills a little past nine-thirty. I blinked my lights twice at the deputy whose cruiser was partly hidden by the live oak. After I parked, I went over to speak to Deputy Dorsey, and thanked him for spotting the abandoned Cadillac. He beamed proudly.

Upstairs, I put the .357 on the counter, and checked the answering machine. Balls had left a message telling me to call him to let him know I was back at the house. I glanced at my watch. A bit late, but I knew he'd want me to call.

I told him about my conversation with Mrs. Mellencamp. The fact that Melvin had lied when he said his mother was the one who tipped him off about Lewiston's concern with the ethanol project. I told him she said she didn't even know Lewiston.

Balls said, "Melvin's becoming quite interesting. What do you think he's up to?"

"Maybe nothing. Maybe covering for something else. These are not *big* lies, but you've got to wonder why." I felt tired. "I've thought about all of this too much. I'm going to bed."

"Me, too," Balls said.

I checked on Janey, then covered her cage. I thought about another shower but took two aspirin instead and went to bed. I slept soundly all night and waked at six-thirty Saturday morning. It was already a bright, sunny day. I looked forward to going over to Elly's that night.

I fixed coffee and took a cup down to Dorsey. The phone was ringing as I came up the stairs. I hurried to it, figuring it was Balls and something else had happened. I grabbed the handset and said hello before I even saw that caller ID had been blocked.

"You enjoy the concert last night, buddy boy?" The syrupy accent.

I wanted to scream obscenities at him. I felt my jaw muscles tensing, but I didn't answer. I didn't say anything. I could hear him breathing. Then the phone clicked off. He wasn't taking any chances by staying on the phone too long.

Always something to screw up your day. But I was determined not to let it. Just the same, he seems to know everything I do, where I go. I thought about tonight. I sure as hell didn't want to put Elly in any danger, and for God's sake, not her child. If I go over there, I want a deputy parked on her street, watching the house, maybe following me to and from her place. Christ, this was getting complicated.

Once again, I called Balls to report what had happened. I was sick of this. I told Balls I wanted it to come to a head, have a confrontation.

Balls said, "Maybe this is what he is counting on. Don't do anything stupid."

He agreed he would check with the sheriff about tonight and sending a deputy to follow me. He said, "Hell, don't want you to miss out on a little courtin' with that young Pedersen gal."

"You're a true romantic, Balls." Then I said, "Balls, I looked around carefully last night. I didn't see anyone following me, I didn't see anyone watching, nothing looked suspicious . . . but why the hell doesn't he make his move?"

"Be careful what you wish for," Balls said. "He's still playing, but I think he's getting to the end of his little game. Maybe he's waiting for the right moment, make it look accidental."

"Yeah, and I know what you mean when you say make *it* look accidental. And, hell, Balls, my only involvement was that I happened to be going to do some peaceful fishing at the Boiler and just happened to see Lewiston and this son of a bitch. I haven't been looking for trouble, or to get involved."

Balls said, "True, but remember you went up to meet with that Keller woman just before she was killed. So, in a way, my friend, you did get yourself involved."

"I guess you're right," I said. Weariness was in my voice.

As the day progressed, with the bright sunshine, low humidity, light wind from the west, it was impossible for my spirits not to rise. I went to the boat and cleaned it up a bit, picking out a few leaves that had blown in. Using a long extension cord, I hooked up the battery charger. Hell, weather holds I just might go out tomorrow, I thought. I'll check Fishing Unlimited or TW's and find out if anything's biting up near the Wright Memorial Bridge.

Late that afternoon I showered and shaved, dressed again in khakis, put on a button-down Oxford weave shirt, and even put on socks with my boat shoes. Heck, I was looking spiffy.

At close to five o'clock I was about ready to leave to go over to Elly's. I kept an eye out for one of the deputies to arrive. Exactly at five, a cruiser pulled into the cul-de-sac. I went down to the driveway to speak to him, another young deputy named Riggs whom I had seen around the courthouse.

"Sorry you're having to babysit tonight," I said.

"No problem, sir."

"We'll leave in about five minutes," I said.

I carried the .357 with me, wrapped in its towel. All the way along the Bypass, Deputy Riggs stayed a car or two behind me, but always close enough to move in rapidly if he had to. We drove slightly above the speed limit of fifty. When we swung west toward Manteo, we slowed to forty-five, then thirty-five. On the west side of Manteo I turned left into the road that led toward Elly's. There are two vacant lots before Elly's house, which is at the end of the road. Riggs waved a hand out of his window and pointed to one of the lots. He backed his cruiser in so he could see both ways on the road.

I couldn't help but feel a little foolish. This whole thing was getting out of hand. I didn't like the idea of someone having to watch my backside practically twenty-four-seven. But, maybe Balls was right. Until this thing is over or the guy makes his move, extra care may be warranted. Just the same, it did, deep down, embarrass me.

Late afternoon light softened the surroundings. Only the tops of the tall pine trees around her house were tipped with sun.

And as I pulled my car up close to her house, there Elly was, standing on the porch, hand raised in greeting. I felt good again.

I took her hand lightly. I wanted to hug her but with Deputy Riggs watching, I skipped it. I saw her look toward the Dare County Sheriff's Department cruiser.

She smiled. "I feel like we've got a chaperone."

We went in the living room and I could smell biscuits and pork chops. I suddenly felt very hungry.

Elly said, "Should we take the deputy a pork biscuit."

"Just one," I said, teasing, being happy.

Mrs. Pedersen stuck her head in the living room. "Hi, Harrison. It'll be ready in a minute."

"Smells great," I said.

Even little Martin came out and almost spoke to me. He had a piece of paper in his hand. With a quick movement, he offered me the paper. It had a crayon drawing on it. Two stick figures and a sun in the background and what I took to be water.

"Oh, that's nice, Martin. I really like it."

Elly's face reddened just a touch. "Martin said that is you and me at the beach."

Now, I truly was inordinately pleased. "May I keep it?" I asked Martin. He nodded, then walked, with what looked like pride, back into the kitchen with Mrs. Pedersen.

Those two little worry-lines appeared between Elly's eyebrows. "I've been keeping Martin close to the house. Maybe that . . . that car out there was nothing."

Knowing I wasn't being completely honest, I said, "I've got a feeling it wasn't connected with . . . with our mystery man."

"You mean killer," she said. "Cold-blooded killer, and maybe even a child molester, too."

I nodded and figured it best not to say anything further.

Before we ate, Mrs. Pedersen brought me a large homemade biscuit with a nice chunk of boneless pork chop encased in it. She had it on a stiff paper plate with a paper napkin on the side. "For the deputy outside," she said.

It smelled good and was still very warm. I took the pork biscuit out to Deputy Riggs. He grinned, "Heck, this ain't bad duty a'tall."

When we went into the small dining room off the living room, I said, "Now this is what I call a real Southern meal."

"Hope you like it," Mrs. Pedersen said.

"What can there be not to like? Nice pork chops, home-made biscuits, baby lima beans, pickled beets, sliced tomatoes and some of your homemade applesauce."

"Peach cobbler, too," Elly said, "with peaches Mother put up last summer."

The meal was excellent, as I knew it would be. The peach cobbler was warm, with chewy pastry on the bottom, melting vanilla ice cream on top.

Afterwards, Elly and I sat in the living room. She went into the back for a while to help her mother get Martin ready for bed. She made him come out to tell me goodnight. He nodded at me. "Thank you again, Martin, for the picture. I'm taking it home with me and putting it on the refrigerator."

He gave a trace of a smile and then Elly took his hand and led him into the back of the house. I sat there on the sofa and thought about how nice all of this was. When Elly returned and sat beside me on the sofa, I said, "This is so very nice, Elly."

She said, "This is the way it is supposed to be."

"I know."

"But this is still just sort of, I don't know, make-believe until this, this person is caught and things can get back to normal." She gave her little laugh. "As normal as they ever will be with you."

"Hey, now that's not fair. I'm a shy, mild-mannered man who just pecks away at a word processor."

"Yeah. Right," she said.

"Well, I never *try* to get involved in these things."

"No, you've just got a talent for it."

"Okay, okay. Really, it'll be coming to a head soon and then things will settle down." We both knew I was doing a bit of whistling in the dark.

Later on I said, "I'd better check on Deputy Riggs. Tell him that I'll be leaving soon. See if he needs anything."

When I came back in, I said, "The sky looks great. I think tomorrow will be a good day to exercise my boat a bit. Want to go?"

"We're going over to Plymouth to see Mother's sister right after church." The two little worry-creases came back again between her eyebrows. "I don't think you ought to go out in the boat, Harrison."

"Oh, it'll be all right. Rev the engine a bit. Fish under the bridge. Catch a nice flounder, maybe."

Elly wouldn't let up. She shook her head. "I don't feel good about it."

I'm glad the thought suddenly came to me. "I'll ask Deputy Odell Wright to go with me. He's been wanting to go fishing with me and he's off tomorrow. I'll give him a ring before I go. And I promise I'll be careful."

She managed a slight smile and her shoulders appeared to relax a bit as she sat there beside me. "I'll feel better about it if he's with you."

But even when I got ready to leave and gave Elly a good-night kiss standing away from the front door so we wouldn't be in Deputy Riggs' line of vision, I could tell that she was still worried.

I put my hand on the doorknob. "Now, don't be down, young lady."

"I can't help it, Harrison. I won't feel good about it until you call me tomorrow night and tell me you're safe."

I told her I would be fine. I waved goodbye to her as she stood on the porch. She raised one hand and wiggled her fingers at me, but that worried look was on her face. Deputy Riggs followed me as I drove away.

Chapter Twenty-Seven

When I got home, I thought it might be a bit too late to call Deputy Odell Wright and invite him to go with me. Decided, instead, to do that first thing in the morning.

The night went fine. I woke early Sunday morning to another day of bright sunshine. The westerly breeze had continued so I knew the sound would be nice and high with water pushed out of the rivers. Tides in the sounds and canals are wind-driven. A northeaster lowers the water level in the sounds and canals, but wind from the west or southwest causes them to rise.

Shortly before eight I called Odell Wright and invited him to go with me. I said, "That is unless you're busy helping your brother build that flying machine."

He chuckled. "Man, I'd love to go with you. Not doing a thing here this morning and don't have anything planned."

We agreed to meet at the Wright Shores boat launching area on Bay Drive at ten.

Sometime during the night another deputy had relieved Riggs, and the new deputy—Officer Walters—was preparing to leave when I went down to the boat. I didn't know him, but we greeted one another and I thanked him, asked him if he wanted coffee. He said that would be great. I brought him a cup and then busied myself with the boat. I unhooked the battery charger, checked the oil level and gasoline. The Ranger has a canvas top that folds back. It needs to be folded back in order to fish. It has four bucket seats and room for a fifth person on a bench at the stern. The two aft bucket seats can be removed and their posts inserted into slots either forward or at the stern for easier casting. The boat has an electric troll motor at the bow that can be operated with foot pedals.

I cranked up the front end of the boat trailer, and then started the engine on my Jeep and prepared to back it carefully toward the trailer. Walters came over to assist. He stood at the rear and gave hand signals to me as I backed slowly toward the trailer. I got it in position and lowered and locked the trailer on the Jeep's ball hitch.

I thanked Walters for his help. "No problem, sir," he said. "Now I'm going home and get some sleep. Off until Tuesday."

"Thanks again for staying here," I said.

He drove away and I cut the engine on the Jeep while I went upstairs and got the .357 wrapped in its towel and picked up the black plastic Ranger utility box in the closet in my bedroom. In the box I keep emergency tools, knife, boat registration, and that sort of thing. I always bring the box with me in the boat, along with the handheld radio for transmission and to check on the ever-changing weather. I also brought my cell phone. Automatically I opened the box to make a quick check of the contents and remembered that's where I'd stored my old .32 pea-shooter when Balls lent me the Big Gun. I snapped the lid shut on the box and went downstairs with it, placed it in one of the forward compartments where I kept the anchor and its line. I put the towel-wrapped .357 in the dashboard's port compartment.

I had just started to the utility room at the house-end of the driveway to get my lifejacket and fishing gear when I heard the phone ringing. I got back upstairs before the voicemail machine kicked in.

It was Balls. "Well, you can call your sweetie and tell her not to worry about some weirdo trying to pick up her boy. We got the guy. At least the Southern Shores police did."

"Yeah?"

"There'd been a couple of other reports about a guy in a dark sedan—turned out to be a navy blue Buick—approaching kids in Kitty Hawk and Southern Shores. Southern Shores police hemmed him in on Duck Woods Drive after he'd approached a kid there. Mama called the cops. One was just coming down the street. Got him."

"That's a relief on my mind, too," I said. "I'll call Elly right now before they leave for church." I took a breath. "Hey, Balls, I'm going out in the boat this morning . . ."

"*What?*" His voice was loud.

"Hold on. I've got Odell Wright going with me."

There was silence. "Well, that's a bit better, anyway. I guess that'll be all right."

"Yeah, I'm not going to stay hostage here. But I figured it'd be best to have someone with me." I gave a short laugh. "Don't want to be like one of my editors described a character in an article of mine—TSTL."

"Huh?"

"TSTL. Too Stupid To Live."

He actually laughed. "Yeah, like in one of those B-grade horror flicks and the teenagers walk into a suspect's house . . . and never turn on the lights."

"Okay, I'll call you when I get back. Now I got to call Elly and give her the good news about the suspected child molester."

I caught Elly just as they were getting ready for church. She sighed and said her prayers were answered. She sounded relieved, too, when I told her that I was meeting Odell Wright and he was going with me in the boat.

I had just gone back downstairs to the utility room and taken gear to the boat, when who pulls into the cul-de-sac in his Camry but Melvin Mellencamp.

Oh, shit. I didn't want to have to fool with him. He squeezed out of his Camry and waddled over to the boat. He wore a striped sport shirt, yellow shorts low on his belly, and what looked like brand new sockless sneakers.

"Wow, all hooked up and ready to go, huh?"

"I thought I might go out for a short spin."

"Hey, let me go with you."

I made something of a face. "I don't know, Melvin."

"Aw, come on. I'm thinking about buying a boat and this would be a good chance to see how an expert handles one."

"I'm no expert, Melvin. I was going to do maybe a little fishing under the Wright Memorial Bridge. Just out for a little while."

"Great. I'd like to watch that. I won't get in your way. I promise."

I figured what the hell. This might be a good time to find out a bit more why Melvin had been telling those lies, not big ones, but lies nonetheless. "Well, okay. Let me get the rest of my fishing gear and a lifejacket for me and for you. And Deputy Wright. He's going with us."

For an instant, a cloud of doubt or concern seemed to flicker across Melvin's face. Then he smiled. "I really appreciate it," he said.

Melvin and I were getting into the Jeep when my cell phone chirped. I flipped it open. It was Odell. "Man, I'm so sorry but the dispatcher just called me. I gotta go on duty. Relieving a deputy who called in sick. I was hoping to catch you before you left."

I told him I was really sorry he couldn't make it. And I was. Well, at least I had good ol' Melvin Mellencamp with me.

I took one of the rods, the one I was going to offer to Odell, back to the utility room. I wasn't going to bother taking one for Melvin.

When I got back to the Jeep, Melvin was just signing off on his cell phone. He grinned, "Like to keep my mother informed as to where I'm going."

I nodded.

We eased out of the cul-de-sac with the trailered Ranger, turned right and headed to a boat ramp on the sound. When we got there and I pulled around to back the boat onto the ramp, Melvin got out to watch for me. I usually place my hand at the bottom of the steering wheel to back a trailer. That way the trailer turns the same direction my hand moves. I'm not a real expert at it.

We got the boat unhitched, secured against the walkway, and I pulled the Jeep and trailer out of the way into a parking area. Melvin was puffing a bit and had already started to sweat, even though it really wasn't that warm yet. But the sun was out, the wind was down and the sound had only dimples of waves on it.

I handed Melvin a lifejacket. I had to adjust it to fit his girth. "These inflate automatically when you pull this cord. Don't pull it unless you're in the water."

"They're trim, aren't they?" he said.

The jackets are trim but with one on Melvin he looked more than ever like a Thanksgiving turkey ready for the roaster.

I told Melvin not to step on the gel finish along the gunwales. He had an awkward time getting aboard. Since it had been a while since I'd started the engine, I used the manual choke at first, then eased off of that, let the motor idle a bit, revved it a couple of times out of gear, then nudged into reverse, eased out of the slip, turned around, and shifted into forward. I kept it at no-wake speed until we were completely clear of the loading area. I looked around. No other boat traffic, which really wasn't all that unusual this time of year. Melvin sat in the passenger seat on the port side. I told him, "Hang on," and I pushed the throttle full forward. The engine revved up to more than 4,000 rpm, the bow came up, then settled nicely into plane and I eased the throttle back to 3,100 rpm. The boat skimmed along smoothly.

"Wow," Melvin said.

I checked the depth finder. The sound is not deep. Three or four feet and even less close to shore. In the channels near Wright Memorial Bridge, where we were headed, the water can be up to nine feet deep. It took us a few minutes to get within sight of the bridge, and about twelve minutes to begin approaching it.

When we got close, I eased back to 1,000 rpm, and idled up to the bridge, deciding to go under it and fish back into the light breeze. When we went under the bridge I could hear the heavy sound of vehicular traffic overhead.

As I gently maneuvered the boat around to nose toward the concrete pilings of the bridge, I saw out of the corner of my eye that Melvin was fooling with the AM/FM radio and CD player in front of him. "Got any CDs in here?" he said, and opened the compartment in the dashboard before I could tell him not to. He saw the towel-wrapped .357. "I see you got your Python with you."

"Don't mess with that," I said.

"I know weapons," he said.

"Then you know not to fool with them."

He smiled, but it was not the chubby, almost boyish smile. It was something else, a slightly different Melvin Mellencamp. He shrugged and closed the compartment.

I decided that with Melvin along I would not try to do any serious fishing by sitting forward and using the trolling motor. Instead I would get closer to the pilings, to the west of the center section of the bridge, put the anchor out, drift with the wind but stay within casting distance of the pilings where I had the best luck. Still drifting slowly toward the pilings, I cut the motor and stepped forward to drop the anchor, shortening the line by securing it around one of the cleats. I moved back and got my rod. I was using a light spinning outfit and an all-purpose jig with a single hook and floppy plastic tail that vibrated when pulled through the water.

The first cast was perfect. The lure fell inches from the concrete piling. I let the lure sink an instant and then began to reel in moderately fast, lifting the rod's tip a time or two to give the jig more action. I cast a few more times and then figured now was the time to begin with a few questions to Melvin. I had moved forward again and I was turned halfway toward him. "Hey, Melvin," I said, "I called Jean Clayborne the other day and she said they didn't have any word about your being rehired by Hand Gun."

"Checking up on me?"

Hearing the tone, I turned my head toward him, still cranking the reel. "Just curious," I said, "and wondering why you told me you were going back with them."

He forced a quick smile that didn't reach his eyes. He shrugged. "When I'm ready," he said.

I cast again. This time the lure smacked against the piling. I retrieved it quickly and cast again. I felt the boat rock slightly as Melvin hoisted himself and stood watching me cast, his arms on the top of the windshield.

A boat approached us from the north from Martin's Point. A man and woman were aboard. The man stood at the console and waved as they slowed slightly to go under the bridge at the raised center section. I leaned a leg against the storage compartment to steady myself against his wake. My boat rolled gently when the swells reached us.

I thought I would push Melvin a bit more. "You know I met your mother last night before the concert. Very pleasant lady."

"Yeah, she said she met you. Said you seemed very nice." His voice was somewhat flat, as if he waited for something else to be said.

I cast again, in the center between the pilings. I started retrieving. Something hit the lure, but didn't get hooked. I reeled in and cast again in almost the same place. "Melvin, she said she didn't even know Carter Lewiston. You told me they were good friends. And that's how you found out there might be something not on the up-and-up about the ethanol project." I glanced at Melvin. A flash of anger crossed his face for an instant and then was gone. But it was there when I first looked.

"Sounds like you *are* trying to check up on me," he said, his eyes trained hard at me.

"I can't help but wonder why you told me these things. And since we're playing the truth game, Jean Clayborne said she heard the Congressman fired you." I held the rod, the line looped over my index finger, ready to cast again but I wanted to see Melvin's reaction.

His voice went stony, as if it had lost all animation. His eyes took on a different hue and narrowed. He appeared ready to respond to me. But then his cell phone rang and he pulled it out of his belt. He had to lean to one side to get his phone because of the lifejacket. His eyes never left me. "Yes?" he said into the phone. Then, "Hello, Mother. We're at the bridge now." There was a pause and then he said, "Good," and flipped the phone off, pushed it back onto his belt.

I cast out again, not really concentrating on where the lure landed.

I pushed him again. "You said you thought the Congressman might have set this whole thing in motion. Was that a little stretching of the truth, too, Melvin?"

I got a sharp strike on the lure, pulled back quickly to set the hook, but the fish was gone. I missed him again.

I sensed some movement from Melvin and turned to look at him. He was staring off to the south, the direction we had come from, watching the approach of another boat. A slight smile was on his lips.

Then, suddenly, with a chill, I knew what the movement had been. He had opened the compartment and had his hand inside. He had the .357. But what made a cold, heavy dread come over me was what he said with a voice that didn't even sound like it was coming from him, like it was the voice of another being.

In a syrupy Southern accent, he said, "Well, buddy boy, you've been doing a whole lot of thinking. Probably too much for your own good. Too much thinking can be deadly, buddy boy."

I stared at him in disbelief. I felt like an icy cold fist gripped my guts. It was the voice from the telephone calls. A perfect mimic.

The boat to the south was coming full-throttle toward us.

Chapter Twenty-Eight

Melvin held the .357 almost casually by his side. Then he motioned to me with it. "Why don't you just have a seat right there on that locker," he said.

I hesitated a moment, not sure what my next move should be.

"Just sit, buddy boy." That accent again. It was eerie. His talent for mimicking a voice didn't stop with members of Congress.

I remained standing. "Then it was you on the telephone," I said, my voice sounding strange to me.

"Not every time," he said, his voice more normal now. "My colleague made a call or two, also."

"Colleague? What the hell's going on, Melvin? What the hell have you got yourself into?"

He gave a slight, phony sounding chuckle. "I don't want to be the underpaid fat boy on a Congressman's staff all my life, or the butt of jokes at Hand Gun. Told you I wanted some of the finer things—a boat, bigger than this one, maybe a nice Cadillac . . . a midnight blue one." He actually winked.

"Your colleague? You mean the psycho killer in the Cadillac who murdered Lewiston and Partens—and Tracy?"

"That was really unfortunate about Tracy. I'll tell you, Weav, I felt awful about that. What do they say? Collateral damage. Hell of a phrase isn't it? But it does happen."

I said, "Money, Melvin? You got involved in this for money? Jesus Christ, man."

He just shrugged.

I did not try to move closer to him. With Melvin holding that gun I wasn't going to try anything fancy. I even thought for a moment of diving overboard. But I knew I'd have a fist-size hole in my back before I could swim three strokes.

Melvin's gaze went again to the approaching boat. In between the roar of vehicular traffic on the bridge, I couldn't begin to hear the boat's engine. The way it was moving, though, I knew I'd be able to hear it in a minute or so. We were close enough to the bridge's pilings that no one driving on the bridge couldn't see us.

Melvin kept his left arm on top of the windshield. His right held the .357. He motioned with the gun as he spoke, as one might gesture with the palm of a hand. "Money? Of course money. That grant, you don't think that was the brainchild of the Congressman, did you? He doesn't have the smarts to do the work involved in that. I did. I did it all."

I thought maybe the lone man in the boat would be able to help. I wanted to keep Melvin talking. "Partens? Was he in on this too?"

"Oh, not in the beginning. He got wind of it when Lewiston started running his mouth. Partens wanted in on the money. My colleague promised him that he would be taken care of." Melvin appeared to think the play on words was funny. He said, "Early on Lewiston had called the Congressman. I took the call and promised Lewiston we'd take care of it." He gave that snorting-like chuckle again. "Yeah, we took care of it."

I glanced over my shoulder at the other boat, which had idled back and begun slipping in between the pilings, edging toward us.

Melvin got that half-smile back on his pig face. "Might as well quit thinking that's help arriving, Weav." He raised his left hand in greeting to the other boater. "That's my colleague."

I may have said, "Shit." It would have been a word called for.

Melvin said, "You don't really think that was my mother I called on the phone before we left, do you? My colleague and I have to stay in touch."

As the boat, a Grady White with a center console, pulled along side, engine idling, I stared at the man at the wheel. It was him, all right. The guy from the beach, the guy who had waved at me twice, the guy who did drive the Cadillac. The killer. The mystery man himself.

The two boats bumped gently. He had cut his engine. Using a boathook, he held his boat fast to the starboard side of mine. The gentle breeze and flow of water helped paste the boats together.

"Hello, buddy boy," he said in that polished Southern accent. "Sorry we haven't been formally introduced before now. But I do believe we've become somewhat acquainted with one another. You can call me Jason, like Jason Compson, one of Faulkner's less desirable characters. Or Shelby. Lot of people say I sound just like the late Shelby Foote, you know who did some of the narrations in Ken Burns' Civil War series?"

He did, indeed, but I said, "I can call you a son of a bitch is what I can call you."

"Now, there you go again, using that gutter language and calling me vulgar names." He wore dark glasses, and what looked like doeskin gloves, a nice shirt and dress khaki slacks. A Greek fisherman's cap set jauntily on his head. He looked more Palm Beach than Outer Banks.

He spoke to Melvin. "Please help me out here, Melvin, if you would. Take the boathook you have on board and help keep these boats together, although I do believe the breeze is aiding us considerably, especially since Mr. Weaver has his boat anchored quite nicely."

Melvin looked around the boat.

"It's right there behind you, Melvin. That long thing with the hook on it like the one I'm holding."

"I see it. I see it."

Melvin took the boathook to the starboard side. The boat listed a bit because both of us stood on the starboard. Melvin hooked onto the Grady White gunwale with one hand. He kept glancing at me, keeping the gun aimed generally in my direction. I tried to watch both of them at the same time, trying to figure what in the hell I could do.

Jason or Shelby, whatever his name was, and I doubted if it was either of those, held to his boathook with one hand and stretched behind him to retrieve a long-barrel pistol from the compartment under the wheel. At a glance I couldn't tell whether it was a .22 with a silencer, but that's what I figured it was.

"That's good, Melvin. Now just hand me that mammoth weapon you're holding."

"What for?"

"Now, Melvin, don't be difficult. We don't want any weapons on Mr. Weaver's boat. That's a nice boat, incidentally. Sure it's not up for sale?" He smiled at me. Then his voice got a bit harder. "Come on, Melvin. Lean over carefully, hold the gun by the barrel and hand it over very easily."

"But. . . ."

"Melvin."

"Okay, okay." Melvin leaned on the gunwale, the boat listed even more, and he handed over the gun, grip first. Jason laid his boathook aside to take the .357. He then laid the .22 on the seat behind him.

I said, "That was a mistake, Melvin."

Melvin wheeled toward me. "What do you know, huh?"

"You think he's going to let you go? Share the money with you?"

A shadow of fear crossed Melvin's face, then was gone. "He's my colleague."

"Yeah, right," I said. "That son of a bitch's got no colleagues."

Jason shook his head sadly. "I do wish you would clean up your language." He hefted the weight of the .357. "My, this is a powerful weapon. Like a cannon. I much prefer a smaller caliber. Does the job without so much, you know, mess."

Melvin held on to the boathook, arm extended, but moved back a step as if he had begun to have doubts.

Jason said, "Now, here's the plan—"

"I can tell you what his plan is, Melvin. He plans to kill us both."

"I do wish you wouldn't interrupt." Since he now had one free hand he picked up the boathook again and secured it to the Ranger's gunwale, holding the .357 down by his side in his left hand. "As I was saying, here's the plan . . ."

My mouth was dry but I felt cold perspiration running down my sides again.

Jason used his thumb to pull back the hammer on the .357.

Melvin shifted his weight from one foot to the other, licked his lips.

Slowly, Jason raised the .357. It was not pointed directly at Melvin's chest, but the barrel kept coming up. Jason held his arm with a slight crook at the elbow. The gun now pointed at Melvin's chest. "The plan is, Mr. Weaver here shoots you with his big gun, and he gets blamed for your death. But you had just enough fight left in you to get off a couple of shots from the .22 that has been used in those other unfortunate occurrences."

Melvin tried to smile, even tried to give a little laugh but it sounded more like a frog croaking. "Now you're kidding, right? You're just kidding? Making sort of a game or something." Melvin dropped the boathook and stepped back against the port gunwale. "Oh, Christ, you're not . . . you're not. . . ."

A heavy truck crossed the bridge, its rumble loud and steady.

That's when Jason fired. Still the noise was loud, deafening. The big slug hit Melvin in the center of his chest and he went over backwards off the side of the boat as if smacked with a giant baseball bat.

My ears rang from the gunshot. As stupid as it sounds, I thought about the fact that Melvin hadn't pulled the cord to inflate his lifejacket. He floated just below the surface, blood pooling out in the water around him.

Almost casually, Jason tossed the .357 into the Ranger, landing with a heavy thud on the deck between the driver's seat and the backbench. With the same graceful movement, he picked up the .22 from the seat behind him and aimed it toward me.

Smiling, Jason said, "Don't even think about it, Mr. Weaver. I'd have to shoot you before you took one step."

I froze there, leaning against the forward compartment. I knew I had to make a move, but what, I didn't know.

"Now, what I'd like you to do, Mr. Weaver, is hoist that anchor. I believe that's the nautical term you Outer Banks residents use. Then stow it in that compartment you're leaning against."

I had no choice, I figured, but to do what he said. I half-knelt on the deck by the locker. Hand-over-hand, I began to bring in the anchor, slowly, keeping my eyes on Jason.

"That's right, Mr. Weaver. Nice and easy so these boats stay coupled together—for the time being." The last couple of yards of the anchor line are chain. I tried to keep the chains from marring the gel coat. Yeah, I thought, now's the time to take good care of this boat's finish.

Then I remembered the Ranger utility box in the compartment that contained my peashooter. Just maybe. . . .

I laid the anchor forward of the compartment lid. I opened the hatch on the compartment, the lid up toward Jason. I knelt on the deck and pretended to carefully coil the anchor line into the compartment. My hands were wet from handling the line. I noticed, too, that my hands were shaking.

Jason said in that syrupy voice, "A little nervous, Mr. Weaver?"

"Fuck you."

"My, my for a writer you really should work on improving your vocabulary."

I was bent over the compartment, stowing the line. But I wanted to keep him talking. "You've got your money now, Jason, or whatever your name is. Nobody knows who you are, why don't you just cut out?" I knew that was not what he planned, but I figured it might give me a moment longer.

"Ah, yes, the money. More like one million two hundred thousand. That's more than just *the money*."

Another loud truck went over the bridge and I unsnapped the latch on the utility box, hoping he couldn't hear it, and reached my hand in and palmed the .32. I trembled and tried to keep it under control.

"Now, stand up, please, Mr. Weaver."

It had to be now.

I crouched as if getting ready to stand, but with a sudden movement flexed my leg muscles with all the strength I had and dived from that half-crouched position toward the deck between the two forward seats. I hit on my chest and arms, the little .32 held in my right hand. At the same time I heard the puff sound of his pistol. It was not loud at all. I felt a sting in my left shoulder I thought was from the way I landed. Then I heard another shot from his pistol and two more in succession. The partially wraparound windshield on the starboard side had a spider-webbed hole in it, and I heard one of the bullets thwack into my driver's seat above me.

I had pulled back the hammer on the .32 and I raised enough to get off a quick shot at him, ducked back down. Another of his rounds clipped the gel coat on the gunwale above me just as I went down flat on the deck again. The Grady White rode higher in the water than my boat, so I knew he had the advantage. I scooted forward slightly, scrunched up against the aft bench, raised quickly and fired again, the .32 having more kick than I expected, and louder.

I think I hit him. He made a sound like I had punched him in the stomach.

My left shoulder stung like a wasp had gotten to me. Then I noticed blood was on my lifejacket and running across my chest. It still didn't hurt, just stung and tingled.

I tried to shoot at him again. I pulled the trigger and the hammer just clicked. I pulled it again. Another misfire from that old ammunition. The big .357 was over to my right. I reached out for it and another of his shots zinged just over my head. But I got the .357, took in a deep breath and raised just enough that I was able to see him. I twisted into a very awkward half-sitting position and aimed the .357, trying to hold it with both hands. But my left arm was useless, I realized, not responding at all.

As I raised, he fired but his pistol was aimed high like he was shooting at something over the top of the boat.

My finger pressed against the trigger as I took aim square on his chest. But I didn't squeeze it off.

His head lolled back and forth like he was trying to shake something off. Then I saw that he began to sag. He reached his free hand behind him to try to steady himself on the console. But his hand slipped off the console and he kept sagging, his legs appearing to lose all of their strength.

He crumpled over backwards.

I stood up so I could see him. He wasn't moving and blood pulsed out of his chest. He gave a slight cough, twice, and then was completely still.

My hands shook. The .357 felt very heavy but I continued to point it at him in case he moved. He wasn't moving. I started to reach my left hand for my radio in the cup holder. But my left arm didn't want to do right. I tucked the gun between my knees and reached for the radio.

I turned the volume up and pressed the transmit button on the side. I had never called the Coast Guard before. I clicked to number 16 and said, "Mayday. Mayday. Shooting at Wright Memorial Bridge. Two dead." A static-crackled voice said, "Copy. Received. Help on the way. Are you all right?" I said I was hurt but I didn't know how bad. The voice repeated, "Help on the way. Help on the way. Do you copy?"

"Yes," I said, but I'd forgotten to push in the transmit button. I put the radio on the deck, and took the .357 in my hand again.

The two boats stayed close together, and both drifted slowly northward away from the bridge. I got onto the aft bench, leaned on the gunwale, still holding the .357 pointed toward the other boat. I had to keep blinking my eyes to make them focus. I glanced down at the lifejacket and thought about how difficult it was going to be to get all of the blood off of it, and now there was blood on the deck, too.

I don't know how long it was and at first I thought it was a whirring sound only in my ears but then I knew it was the sound of a helicopter. Obviously one of the Coast Guard choppers had been close by practicing rescue operations. It began to circle low overhead. Using a bullhorn, one of the crew leaned out of the side door of the helicopter and bellowed in a mechanical voice, asking if I was all right. I waved. I remembered I had the gun in my hand, so I put it down and waved again.

The bullhorn again. "Help is on the way. We're staying with you."

Maybe I dozed a moment. I'm not sure. I know I was very tired and sleepy. Then two boats appeared, then a third. Two were police boats and one was someone I knew from the Coast Guard Auxiliary.

The police boarded, weapons drawn. Two officers had boarded the Grady White. I heard one of them yell to the sergeant on my boat, "He's dead." The other officer on my boat was a medical technician and he began to examine my shoulder.

And I wanted to go to sleep.

But before I drifted off, I remember telling the officer, "My boat's a mess."

Chapter Twenty-Nine

I was in and out of consciousness and I can't remember all of the details until I woke up in what I knew was the emergency room at the little Outer Banks Hospital, and a nurse named Donna was asking me if I was awake. Donna wouldn't give me any water to drink but she did give me some crushed ice. There was a lot of activity outside the small room I was in. My shirt was off and I was half-way into one of those hospital gowns. An IV was attached to my right arm with two bags on it. While I was watching the drip from the IV I went back to sleep.

Later on I waked again and Balls was standing there. When he saw me open my eyes, the frown left his face. He gave that old Tom Selleck grin. "Well, you got the son of a bitch."

"My boat's a mess," I said.

"Looks like you got Melvin, too," he said. "They fished him out of the sound. He was shot with a big gun."

"The other guy did it," I said. My voice sounded thick, the words slurred a bit.

"I figured you did it. Melvin was in on it. Got that pretty much confirmed earlier today from Hilda Walston. She and Congressman Walston are both down here this weekend."

"He was in on it all right," I said. "The other guy wanted it to look like we killed each other." As I tried to look at Balls, he went out of focus a bit and I had to blink my eyes.

"You may have to work at it a bit to convince Schweikert that the other guy shot Melvin. Doesn't make that much difference, anyway. Self-defense if nothing else," Balls said.

"I didn't shoot him. Other guy did."

"Jason Shelby," Balls said. "That's his name. We've already confirmed it."

"Sumbitch telling the truth then about his name."

"And Hilda, backed up by the Congressman, acknowledged that her brother was trying to get in on it, too. But they think Melvin is really the one who started it. That's the reason Walston fired him."

"Melvin was in on it, awright," I said.

"You sound drunk," Balls said.

"My boat's a mess."

Donna came back into the room. "We've got to roll you down to X-ray now," she said.

"I'll be back later," Balls said. He turned to leave, stopped and looked back at me. "Not that it makes any difference now, but that suspected pedophile got picked up in Southern Shores? He confessed to trolling around Southern Shores and Kitty Hawk. Said he'd never been to Manteo. So maybe that guy who approached the Pedersen kid was really . . . but no sense in mentioning now."

I nodded. "No sense," I mumbled.

After Balls left, Donna had me wheeled down to X-ray. When I came back she gave me more pain medication. The shoulder had begun to really hurt. The medicine made me feel even more loopy. I probably dozed again. But I was awake and propped up in bed when Elly came hurriedly into the room that evening. Like Balls, she had a worried look on her face until she saw that I was awake and winked at her.

Her smile was big. She leaned over and kissed me lightly on the lips. She smelled good, as always, like fresh cotton and sunshine.

She held my right hand and squeezed it.

"My boat's a mess," I said. I don't know why I kept repeating that, but it came out again.

She got her crooked smile to her lips. "And you're a mess," she said. She patted down the front of my hair with her free hand. "You look like you got caught in high tide."

"I love to hear you talk," I said.

"That's the reason I said 'hoigh toide' for you." She shook her head but she was still smiling. "Yes, Harrison, you got yourself tumbled by the tide's overwash."

"Almost," I said.

Those two little worry creases appeared between her eyebrows. "I was so scared when I heard you were hurt. So scared."

"Me, too," I said. Then I managed a fairly decent smile. "My boat's a mess."

EPILOGUE

I probably would have been released from the hospital on Monday, but they wanted my regular physician to check me out first and he was out of town until Monday night. The X-rays determined that the bullet had only chipped a bit of bone and had then gone cleanly through the muscle and tissue. They put new dressings on the wound, gave me a couple of prescriptions. My arm was put in a temporary sling, and they sent me on my way Tuesday morning, with an appointment to see my doctor again on Thursday. Balls came to the hospital to drive me home.

Naturally there was the legal stuff. I was interviewed by Balls and his supervisor, and Schweikert had me sit in his office with another attorney and court reporter who took a deposition as to what had happened. Schweikert was actually almost polite to me, although he did make a snide comment about how I always got myself connected to deaths. I think the toughest thing to convince them of was that I wasn't the one who shot Melvin Mellencamp.

It helped that Congressman Walston executed a written statement saying that he fired Melvin because he was suspicious that Melvin was linked to a scam to get his hands on the grant money. Melvin's involvement never really became public, and I'm glad for his mother's sake. The fact that Partens was trying for a chunk of the money never came out either. And that's just as well. I really believe that sometimes it's best just to let ghosts drift off and never call them back again.

The man I killed, Jason Shelby, was originally from Alabama and was linked to a number of killings for hire, although his record was relatively clean. He had managed to do disappearing acts, only to reappear in a different location. I could attest to that.

The money from the grant? Officials are still trying to retrieve the half that Jason skimmed off, most of which he stashed in a bank over in the islands. Eventually they say they'll get it back.

Gifford Grudgeon and the others are determined to go ahead with the ethanol project, and say that it will be an economic boon to Northeast North Carolina.

Balls was pleased to eventually get his Python .357 back, rather quietly from one of the deputies. Balls told me to get rid of that peashooter, but I think I'll hold on to it, maybe buy some fresh ammo.

I'm still dealing with the insurance company about the damage to my boat, including cleaning up the blood I got all over the rear deck and bench seat. The boat's over in Wanchese for the repairs. An exasperated claims agent at the insurance company said they had never had to deal with a gun battle aboard one of their insured boats.

It's been three weeks now since that Sunday. It feels like summer is really here, and I'm ready to enjoy it. To get my shoulder back to normal, I'm doing physical therapy with Amy up at Outer Banks Physical Therapy at Martin's Point.

Typing mostly with one hand, I've used these three weeks to finish the last of the book and send it electronically to my editor. Just last week the editor called with another project she said should be a book deal—the mysterious death of a female government worker who was found nude and hogtied in the backseat of her government car in the mountains of North Carolina.

But, I don't know.

I mentioned it to Elly last night when I was over there, and promised her I would think long and hard about it before I committed.

When I kissed her goodnight and pulled her up against me there in the living room, I repeated what had become a standing joke between us. I said, "One of these days. . . ."

She got a smile on her face like she had something planned. "At the rate you are going, getting caught up in these things that turn out to be so dangerous, maybe we'd better really work on that 'one of these days' and move those days up closer."

So I'm sort of walking on cloud nine. It's now Sunday evening and I'm going over to Elly's for supper. She'll be standing on the front porch, one hand raised, wiggling her fingers in greeting.

And I'll smile and think to myself, "One of these days. . . ."

The End

About the Author

Joseph L.S. Terrell makes his home on the Outer Banks of North Carolina, his native state, where he continues the craft of fiction-writing—with a little fishing, golfing and boating thrown in.

He may be reached through Bella Rosa Books or via email at JLSTERRELL@aol.com.

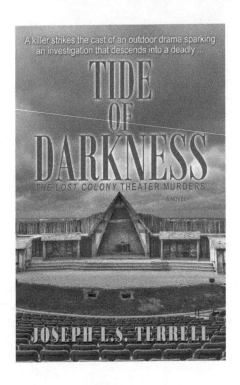

TIDE OF DARKNESS

The Lost Colony Theater Murders

ISBN 978-1-933523-66-8

True-crime writer Harrison Weaver arrives at North Carolina's picturesque Outer Banks seeking peace and quiet. But his resolve to avoid even thinking about murder is dashed when he discovers, on the night of his arrival, that the body of another young female cast member of *The Lost Colony* outdoor drama has been found strangled and thrown into Croatan Sound—a killing eerily similar to an unsolved case that first brought Weaver to the Outer Banks four years earlier. Despite his promise to himself, Weaver is drawn into the investigation—only to find that he may be the killer's next victim.

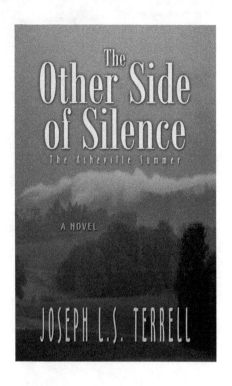

The Other Side Of Silence

The Asheville Summer

ISBN 978-1-933523-10-1

That summer in the mountains near Asheville, North Carolina, between the end of the Great Depression and the onset of World War II promised to be an enchanted one for ten-year-old Jonathan Clayton and his family. But almost from the beginning, Jonathan sensed that something sinister lived across the meadow at the base of Clown Mountain in the Dennihan's pigpen of a house. Before the summer ended, violence erupted in that house and Jonathan, his brother, sister, and cousins have to race ahead of a crazed, hatchet-wielding mountain man in a frantic flight to save their lives and stop their pursuer—by any means they can.

CPSIA information can be obtained
at www.ICGtesting.com
Printed in the USA
BVHW060538021021
617948BV00002B/154